D0886899

The Urewera Notebook

The
Urewera
Notebook

KATHERINE
MANSFIELD

Edited with an Introduction
by Ian A. Gordon

Oxford University Press

1978

Oxford University Press
Oxford London Glasgow New York
Toronto Melbourne Wellington Ibadan
Nairobi Dar es Salaam Lusaka Cape Town
Kuala Lumpur Singapore Jakarta Hong Kong
Tokyo Delhi Bombay Calcutta Madras Karachi

Introduction, editorial arrangement, and notes: © 1978 Ian A. Gordon

Text of the notebook: © 1978 Estate of Katherine Mansfield
Some parts of the notebook have been previously published in:
Journal of Katherine Mansfield, *copyright 1927 Alfred A. Knopf Inc.,*
renewed 1955 J. Middleton Murry
and in:

Life of Katherine Mansfield, *1933, by R. E. Mantz; published by*
Constable & Company Ltd., London; Oxford University Press, Bombay, Calcutta,
Madras; Macmillan Company of Canada Ltd., Toronto.

Acknowledgements:
The text of the notebook is reproduced by arrangement
with the Society of Authors as the literary representative of the Estate of
Katherine Mansfield, and the Alexander Turnbull Library, Wellington.
The photographs and the manuscript facsimiles are reproduced by the kind
permission of the Alexander Turnbull Library.

This book is copyright.
Apart from any fair dealing for the purpose of private
study, research, criticism or review, as permitted under the Copyright Act, no
part may be reproduced by any process without the prior permission of the
Oxford University Press

ISBN 0 19 558033 8 CLOTH
ISBN 0 19 558034 6 PAPER

Phototypeset in Bembo and printed by
Whitcoulls Limited,
Christchurch

Robert Manning Strozier Library

JUL 2 1980

Tallahassee. Florida

Contents

List of Illustrations

KM at the time of the Urewera notebook.
A family snapshot Wellington 1907: KM and her brother Leslie.
The little boy she is holding is her young nephew Brian Derry.

Introduction

Katherine Mansfield: the Wellington Years,
a Reassessment

– 1 –

KATHERINE MANSFIELD lived in Wellington for a total of sixteen years, just under half her lifetime. She was born there, and she was sent to three Wellington schools, each a step up the social and educational ladder. Her father, Harold Beauchamp, ambitious for his daughters and well able to provide for them, made a decision to further the process by placing them in a school in England. From April 1903 till July 1906, KM[1] and her two older sisters lived as boarders in Queen's College, Harley Street, London. They returned to Wellington at the end of that year.

KM in 1906 was no schoolgirl. She was a young woman of eighteen of considerable determination, equipped with the skills, the experiences, and the tastes that had been rapidly developed in these four formative years in London. She had become a competent musician (in love, too, with a young professional musician), a keen concert-goer. She knew the London art galleries; she had been to the opera and to those new performances (for which the word 'cinema' had not yet been invented); she could write with some competence both French and German; she was widely read in English, totally immersed in the literature of the 'decadent' nineties. She had even written a section of a novel. Whether it was to be her cello or the manuscript of *Juliet* that would lead to the next step, she had not yet decided. But one thing she did know, when she returned to

Wellington in 1906, that she would not be there for long, in this small, distant, colonial town. She exerted pressure on her family to allow her to return to London. It took her a year and a half before she finally departed, in July 1908. Her writing career – and her later reputation – were still in the future.

This bald account of the external facts is well known. It has all the makings of the standardized story of the young writer of promise who breaks with family and home to struggle towards accomplishment and ultimate recognition. It is, with greater detail, what emerges from the accounts written by all her main biographers. But when one sets this quite conventionally patterned narrative (youthful rebellion justified by adult achievement) against KM's own major work in fiction, we are – or should be – left with a certain disquiet.

If she disliked her birthplace so much, why is it the centre of all her best work? If she rebelled against her Victorian family, why is that family – lovingly remembered – at the core of all her great stories? If the external facts represent the truth, why did she not go on later to write, as other writers of the time did, works that display the painful stresses of Victorian family life, as Gosse did in *Father and Son* and Butler in *The Way of All Flesh*? Why did she, instead, (as she wrote to a friend in 1921) 'try to make family life so gorgeous – not hatred and cold linoleum – but warmth and hydrangeas'?[2]

The life has been told many times. Only three biographers have written of her with scholarly care, R. E. Mantz (1933), S. Berkman (1951), and A. Alpers (1953).[3] The picture that emerges from all three of KM, in her year and a half in Wellington between 1906 and mid-1908, is consistent. She is a moody and disgruntled adolescent at odds

12

with her family. 'Dark thoughts crowded upon her' . . . 'dark moods of restlessness' . . . 'pressure of unhappiness' . . . (Mantz); 'exiled in the wilderness' . . . 'in moody reverie' . . . 'her heart was sick with despair' . . . 'fever of unrest' . . . 'in this season of rebellion' . . . (Berkman); 'outrageous scenes' . . . 'bitterness in her heart' . . . 'to the parents . . . a problem and a social embarrassment' . . . (Alpers). These phrases are a fair representation of the KM of the Wellington years presented by her three most careful biographers. Where, in all this misery, did she find the 'warmth and hydrangeas'?

In view of what evidence was available to them, I do not think the biographers could have come to any other conclusion. It was a reasonable enough inference at the time. Till the late fifties, the 'facts' of her life and attitude could be deduced only from five of her printed books, the *Journal* published in 1927 (and later expanded in 1954), the *Scrapbook* published in 1939, the two volumes of *Letters* published in 1928, and the *Letters to John Middleton Murry* published in 1951. KM had no hand in any of these publications.[4] All five volumes were posthumous, all edited by KM's husband Murry. All were utterly 'authentic' in the sense that – apart from Murry's commentaries – every word in them was written by KM.

They are also utterly unreliable, because (without recourse to the documents from which they have been drawn) one cannot be certain on any page that it has been accurately transcribed, or that what one reads is the whole of what KM wrote, or that what is presented is presented in a sequence that KM herself would have determined. This uncertainty extends even to the edition of the *Journal* of 1954, in spite of the reassurance on the title-page: 'Definitive Edition'.

The evidence for this unreliability is now available, in KM's own papers and notebooks. She wrote, during her lifetime, considerable material which she did not publish. She kept it in notebooks, diaries, sheets torn from writing-pads (pinned together to ensure their sequence), single sheets of paper. The earliest extant notebook was begun in 1903, when she was fourteen; the latest, shortly before her death in 1923. The material is varied. On occasion, she bought a printed pocket diary – and the entries tend to be quite perfunctory 'diary' entries (tapering off towards February). The separate sheets may contain drafts of stories, brief 'story' ideas, poems (sometimes her own, sometimes a copy of verses that had attracted her), 'personal' observations on life and literature (which may or may not be dated). The notebooks have seldom any internal unity of material and certainly no absolute internal 'order'. They are simply her rough working notes. She will make entries at several points in a notebook, filling in the intervening pages at later dates. She will begin a notebook – and then turn it upside-down and 'begin' it again from the 'back'. She will, on occasion, return to an old notebook, re-read it, and add further observations.

The contents of these notebooks can be almost anything: 'diary' entries; clothing lists; household accounts; shopping lists; her sizes in gloves and shoes; brief jottings of 'ideas' for stories; stories in draft form; draft letters (which may or may not have been re-copied and posted); isolated sentences and isolated paragraphs worked up to the 'finished' form in which they appear in her printed works; personal observations on places and people (dated and undated); pages where she is simply thinking aloud; critical observations on her current reading; again and again (usually in the final pages of a diary or notebook) meticulously kept balance-sheets of income and expenditure, entered up with quite professional skill.

KM clearly set great store by this accumulation. Six notebooks were filled before she left New Zealand in 1908. They travelled with her. 'I'm taking', she wrote her sister Vera on 19 June 1908 just before her departure, 'only half a dozen books and my photographs'.[5] The 'books' were her own notebooks. They travelled with her constantly. I have the distinct impression that in all her many shifts from house to house, from country to country – New Zealand, England, France, Italy, Switzerland – her growing pile of notebooks, diaries, and manuscripts went with her, raw material for creation.

In his preface to the 1927 *Journal*, Murry stated categorically that she had destroyed her early 'huge complaining diaries'. He consequently opened the 1927 version of the journal at 1914. I find his undocumented assertion unconvincing. By 1933 Murry had clearly uncovered some of her notebooks written earlier than 1914, and these were disclosed to Mantz, since she used fragments of them in her *Life* of that year. There is also no confirmation, anywhere in KM's own writings, of such wholesale destruction. The passage Murry cites as his sole evidence is an apostrophe to her dead brother ('To whom did I always write when I kept these huge complaining diaries?'[6]) and it says nothing of destruction – indeed 'kept' (for all its ambivalent meaning) suggests the opposite. The appearance in the late fifties of a whole group of pre-1914 notebooks (one of them the subject of this edition) now casts additional doubts on Murry's statement. KM, even when she was re-reading what made her angry or miserable, was a great hoarder of her own papers. 'We can't afford to waste such an expenditure of feeling', she wrote in 1921 to Dorothy Brett.[7] She felt the same about her papers, especially if they contained her past. She could not afford to waste them, with the result that we have them today.

- 3 -

After the death of KM, Murry issued two posthumous volumes of her stories, *The Doves' Nest* (1923) and *Something Childish* (1924). He then turned to the vast accumulation of her notebooks and sheets of paper which he had inherited, and from this – with quite superb editorial skill – he quarried the 1927 *Journal*. The *Journal of Katherine Mansfield* was a best-seller. It remains a remarkable book. But Murry's editorial methods make this beautiful and pious memorial of a dead wife an insecure basis for biography. He discarded, suppressed, edited, and manipulated. He ran together (without indication) 'diary' entries and passages of KM's fiction; dropped in – at what seemed 'appropriate' places – poems which KM had copied out on single undated sheets and which she had no thought of using to reinforce any 'diary' entry. He discarded everything that did not fit in with his presentation of the idealized portrait of a rare spirit.

He discarded her downright enjoyment of New Zealand on her return. He discarded early entries on her 'passion' for the woman artist EKB. He discarded her tough-mindedness; her shrewdness with money; her carefully kept accounts and balance-sheets; her single-minded (on occasion, even ruthless) determination; her jealous bitchiness when she suspected him of having an affair with Dorothy Brett; her very explicit account of *her* affair with the French novelist Francis Carco.[8] His selected and re-arranged

16

material offered instead a romanticized, insubstantial persona who, he wrote, 'seemed to adjust herself to life as a flower adjusts itself to the earth and the sun'.[9]

This central figure of the 1927 *Journal* greatly appealed to the reading public of the day, and it has had a profound influence on later biographical and critical studies. It was not the KM known to her contemporaries. Where in the *Journal* is the KM whom Carrington reported to Lytton Strachey as having 'danced ragtime' at Garsington?[10] Where is the 'forcible and utterly unscrupulous character' recorded by Virginia Woolf?[11] This latter portrait is coloured by openly admitted jealousy. But it cannot be ignored – and it can be found in KM's own notebooks. Lytton Strachey knew her well; had tea with her at Gower Street; acted with her at Garsington; even (for a time) 'she took my fancy a great deal';[12] then changed his mind when he found there was steel behind her mysterious charms. When the 1927 *Journal* appeared, he found it 'incomprehensible'. With his usual combination of spitefulness and acute insight he put his finger infallibly on its contrived falsity. The implications of his comments are inescapable – 'I see Murry lets it out that it was written for publication – which no doubt explains a great deal. But why that foul-mouthed, virulent, brazen-faced broomstick of a creature should have got herself up as a pad of rose-scented cotton wool is beyond me'.[13] Strachey in 1927 had no way of knowing that the masquerade was one in which his old acting-partner KM had no part.

Murry some years later made a further incursion into the paper accumulation he had inherited, transcribing enough to fill another volume, which he entitled the *Scrapbook* (1939). Finally, in 1954, he assembled a revised version of the 1927 journal material; added on considerable portions of the 1939 scrapbook material, and expanded this collection by incorporating a group of 'fragments' (his description)[14] from the pre-1914 notebooks. They are only fragments because of his editorial decision to print fragments from what were well-filled notebooks. This new collection became the 'Definitive Edition' of the *Journal*, published in 1954. In his new preface, he stated that he had restored passages 'suppressed in the original edition'. But his instincts remained: to trim; to excise; to reshape. The notebooks of KM's Wellington years made their first appearance in 1954 heavily edited and consequently distorted. The 1954 *Journal* is as unsecure a basis as the 1927 version on which KM's biographers had been unwittingly compelled to build.

– 4 –

KM's entire accumulation of notebooks and papers became for the first time available on Murry's death in 1957. They were bought at auction by the New Zealand Government and are now in the Alexander Turnbull Library in Wellington. Simultaneously, the library acquired her letters to Murry. The collection was later expanded, notably by the acquisition of his letters to her, of a number of her letters to her contemporaries, and of a considerable group of Beauchamp family documents. From this collection, several early 'Unpublished Writings of Katherine Mansfield' have been printed in the *Turnbull Library Record*, transcribed and edited by Mrs Margaret Scott. The Turnbull collection has brought a new dimension to Mansfield studies. It is now possible to study, from her own drafts and corrections, something of her method of composition. Above all, a more real KM has emerged from behind the partly fictional persona of the *Journal*.

18

The present edition of what I have called the 'Urewera notebook' presents an aspect, so far unrecorded, of KM's New Zealand experience. It is transcribed from what she called a 'Rough Note Book',[15] which she began in Wellington in November 1907 and carried to England in 1908, continuing to write it up in London till the end of that year, concluding it in Belgium in April 1909. KM, in November and December 1907, was one of a party which made an extensive camping trip through the North Island of New Zealand. The first half of the notebook was written during the trip. It forms a detached and self-contained episode.

Murry made no use of the notebook in the 1927 *Journal*. In the 1954 version he presented (pp.22-33) a considerably truncated version of KM's notes on the trip. His text is marred by numerous misreadings (admittedly of a very difficult manuscript, often written on a moving waggon) but also by considerable suppressions and large excisions which result in inevitable falsification. I do not think the falsification is deliberate. Murry in this notebook encountered a KM he had never known, describing a country he had never visited, in a handwriting that even he could only partially decipher. His shortened version of 1954 (only the first part of the trip is attempted), with its misreadings of some words of strategic importance in the narrative, firmly established the conception of KM as an unhappy young woman on her return to New Zealand, miserably trailing her way through a 'loathsome trip' and finding in Rotorua a 'little Hell'. It is no wonder that despair, bitterness and misery have been built on this foundation.

The full text reveals an astonishingly different KM, alertly recording the landscape, visiting bustling sheep-yards, fascinated by the Maoris (especially the Tuhoe people

of the only recently penetrated Urewera country), recording their language with accuracy (even to the extent of using
phonetic script), apart from a few days of sickness (brought
on by Rotorua's rotten-egg smell) vigorously enjoying
herself ('we laugh with joy all day'), sitting on a rock beside
the rapids of the Waikato River imagining that she and her
companions are Wagnerian Rhine Maidens, climbing down
a ladder under the Huka Falls and finding the experience
reminds her of a London production of Tannhaüser,
luxuriating in the hot mineral pools ('happy – blissfully
happy'), finding in the landscape parallels in her reading of
H. G. Wells, Walt Whitman and Maeterlinck, eating rounds
of bread and jam and drinking great pannikins of tea,
revelling in life in a tent ('we are like children here all
happiness'), walking mile after mile uphill to lighten the
load on the horses, writing it all up every night in the tent
and (on occasion) as she sat on top of the luggage in the
baggage-waggon – and bouncing back from the Urewera
adventure to put on, for the benefit of her friend Edie
Bendall (EKB), comic imitations of her travelling companions and of fat old Maori women[16] – and then firmly
setting down in the notebook her clear-cut and organized
programme for her next move – she even enjoyed Rotorua's 'little Hill' – 'Hell' was a Murry misreading.

The Urewera notebook is a key text for an understanding
of the young KM. She was no disgruntled adolescent, but a
young, vigorous, independent-minded woman who saw in
the travelling and camping adventure an opportunity to
expand her experience and to explore a technique of
observation and reportage. Her notebook is not a diary. It is
a writer's notebook, analogous to an artist's sketchbook.
She records, not the day-by-day minutiae of camp life, but
landscapes, characters met by the way, incidents, emotional

reactions. The writing, though in sketchbook form, is deliberate and careful, at times showing significant signs of stylistic revision. Some of it – for a writer of nineteen – I find impressive. Witness her sympathetic portrait of young Johanna, the guide's niece (a 'Mansfield character' in embryo), her reaction to the Urewera bush ('gigantic and tragic even in the bright sunlight'), and the brilliant little steel-engraving of the Maori group at Taupo.

– 5 –

She returned from the camping trip to Wellington in mid-December 1907, confident and full of plans. She left for England six months later. All accounts of KM depict these six months as a time of unhappiness – 'bitter and painful months' (Mantz); 'through late winter and spring she suffered' (Berkman, forgetting or unaware that January and February are, in New Zealand, high summer); 'a fevered mind' . . . 'hysteria' (Alpers). What had happened to the confident and 'blissfully happy' young woman of the Urewera notebook?

Had she, in fact, altered at all? The evidence for an unhappy half-year of self-pity proves, on close examination, to be both minimal and dubious. It consists of two bare items. Ida Baker (LM), her ever-attentive companion in England and Europe, had a memory (nearly half a century old) of a letter she had once received from KM. The letter had long since disappeared. On this basis, Alpers reconstructs a family quarrel as the source of her hysteria. He takes the sensible precaution of prefacing his reconstruction of the scene with the word 'conjecturally'.[17]

The only other evidence ultimately resolves itself into three brief 'diary' entries totalling twelve lines (10 February,

21

18 March, 1 May 1908) first printed in the Mantz *Life*.[18] These have been faithfully re-cited in all subsequent studies. Even Murry, collecting material for the 1954 *Journal*, covered these critical six months by reprinting brief excerpts already printed by Mantz and he made no attempt to supplement them with KM's considerable notebook entries for 1908. There was thus established in 1933 what one might call the 'Mantz portrait', from which all subsequent portraits are derivatives, the KM of the 'bitter and painful months' of 1908. The Mantz portrait has been accepted without examination. It does not match the documents.

KM's notebooks for the period (from which Mantz selected only a few apparently self-dramatizing lines) run to many pages. They are a collection of personal notes, extensive pieces of fiction, sometimes an amalgam of both. The material requires the most careful assessment in context if it is to be used for biographical inferences. The 'heroine' of any particular page is as likely to be a fictional creation, or a literary experiment in the rendering of possible moods, as a self-portrait. These notebooks must be read in the context of documentation that was either not available or, if available, was not fully read and used in the nineteen-thirties. Once again, a very different KM emerges.

The Mantz portrait of KM, the distraught sufferer of the years 1907-8, on which all subsequent versions have been based, has as little foundation as the rare spirit of the *Journal*. The full text of KM's letters of the time, her early notebooks, the testimony of her Wellington contemporaries of her own social group, family documents, school records – almost none of which were accessible until recently – present a quite different picture. KM remained the confident young woman of the Urewera notebook.

When she returned to Wellington, she settled down to a regular routine. She spent hours alone, writing. That is what one expects of a writer. She had by now been published several times in Australia; and the journalist Tom L. Mills (whom Beauchamp had called in to advise her and who was now on a provincial newspaper) printed more of her contributions in his weekly literary supplement.[19] She went on with her preparations for the life ahead; set herself a stiff course of reading at the General Assembly Library; and abandoned her cello for a training more appropriate to a writer. 'My plans', she wrote to her sister Vera, 'they are work and struggle and learn and try and lead a full life and get this great heap of MSS off my hands.'[20]

This is hardly the programme of an unhappy literary recluse. 'Lead a full life'? She threw herself into the life around her – swam in the Thorndon Baths;[21] went walking with her fourteen-year-old brother ('I never dreamt of loving a child as I love this boy');[22] went to the theatre with her family ('to the *Three Little Maids* last night');[23] holidayed with her sister Chaddie at Day's Bay;[24] played billiards at the home of the Prime Minister Sir Joseph Ward (Rubi Seddon, daughter of a Prime Minister, was in the party);[25] attended with Tom Seddon (Rubi's brother) a debate at the university college (to the indignation of the women on the committee who considered that Tom should have squired a properly matriculated student);[26] enjoyed – and coolly rejected – *five* offers of marriage (her italics);[27] engaged in the summertime tennis parties at the family home at 47 Fitzherbert Terrace;[28] danced with the young men of her social group in Wellington with open enjoyment ('I think I am more popular than any girl here at dances');[29] It was, of course, no more than a continuation of the life she had been leading before the camping trip, when the family gave a dance for her nineteenth birthday and showered her with gifts ('Mother gave her greenstone ear-rings, Father two sweet Liberty broaches').[30] It was a life, in the social circle in which she had been brought up, of quite orthodox normality.

The only element in the life of this lively and attractive young woman of nineteen that was neither normal nor orthodox was her steely determination. She was still determined to return and write in London and determined to persuade Harold Beauchamp that her plan was feasible. With only a few sketches and stories in print, she was already on the way to becoming a young professional, coolly observing her material in terms of how it could be utilized and rendered in fiction. After one quite casual (and innocuous) conversation with a visiting musician, she wrote in one of her notebooks 'I'm glad about the whole affair. I shall pervert it – and make it fascinating'. (This comment, excised from the 1954 printed version of the *Journal*,[31] well illustrates the dangers of a simplistic use of her writing as biographical data). In the same notebook, she records of one of her many Wellington admirers 'I am so eternally thankful that I did not allow J— to kiss me . . . I used him merely for copy'.[32] The KM that Virginia Woolf came to know was already in the making. It would not be long before she got her own way in Wellington.

– 6 –

KM went on with her writing – and her planning. Her next move was shrewdly practical. Several of the young men she danced with were taking degrees at the recently founded university college. She, too, could have matriculated. But she had different priorities, and in the autumn quarter of

24

1908 she went back to school. Her fourth Wellington school, the Wellington Technical School, taught plumbing and engineering to the tradesmen of the town; for the leisured ladies of KM's circle (like Tom Seddon's sister May) it offered painting, sculpture, repoussé metal-work. KM did not join the leisured ladies. She paid her guinea (along with some of Wellington's future commercial leaders) to enrol as a student of 'Commercial Subjects', and spent her mornings on typing and book-keeping.[33] It was all calculated, deliberate and organized. She described her programme – that of a hard-working student – to Vera: 'I go to the Technical School every day – Library till five – then a walk – and in the evening I read *and* write'.[34] KM was deliberately, I think, adding some useful skills for the future – later she handled her little Corona typewriter[35] with effect and (a banker's daughter) she always kept careful and balanced accounts.[36] She was also, I think, in the early part of 1908, impressing on her father that she was well able to look after herself.

Beauchamp had, originally, been reluctant to agree to KM's plan to return, on her own, to London. Indeed he had come to regret sending the girls overseas for their schooling. He found he had lost his daughters,[37] and he did not repeat the experiment with the two younger children. Mrs Beauchamp came up with a more acceptable alternative – a flat in London and £300 a year for the three young women.[38] But KM's older sisters had other plans for their future.

Finally, it was all decided. 'There could be no question of standing in her light', Beauchamp wrote in his *Reminiscences*.[39] He settled on her an allowance for the rest of her life.[40] There was a round of farewell parties, culminating in a grand affair at the residence of Sir Joseph Ward, the Prime

Minister; and then KM, 'more popular than any girl here at dances', left it all behind. She sailed in July. The Urewera notebook was in her luggage. Some years later, she set it all down, in a story called 'The Scholarship' – the eager anticipation of going 'off to Europe' mingling with regret at leaving the 'darling, darling little town'.[41] She never forgot (how could she?) Wellington and the warmth and hydrangeas of Fitzherbert Terrace. In 1921 it became the setting for one of her most moving stories, *An Ideal Family*.

When KM arrived in London, in the autumn of 1908, the New Zealand notebooks were for a time laid aside. She had her old associates to link up with and a very different kind of full life to occupy her attention. She had also her writing; but in the competitive London scene, the 'little colonial' (her own phrase)[42] made at first slow headway, only a few oddments finding their way into print. In the early months of 1910, within two years from her arrival, she had made the breakthrough with a story in the *New Age*. Thereafter, she was a regular contributor, and till early in 1912 it published her tartly satirical stories with settings familiar from her recent experiences in England, Belgium and Bavaria. The Bavarian stories, collected in 1911, became her first published volume, *In A German Pension*, twice reprinted and enthusiastically reviewed. This led to a request for a story from an unknown young editor, John Middleton Murry, who had recently started a periodical *Rhythm*. He found her contribution (a 'bitter fairy story') not easy to understand and asked for something different.[43] Though neither knew it, a turning-point had come in their lives.

KM had already, in her search for themes, made a secret return to Wellington. 'A Birthday' (printed in the *New Age* in May 1911) stands apart from the ill-humour that runs

26

through the other stories in *In A German Pension*. Only the names are German. Setting and theme come from her Wellington memories, and the house of Andreas Binzer is recognizably the house of the opening pages of 'Prelude'. It is no accident that it is the one story in *In A German Pension* that radiates warmth. If Murry wanted something different from what she had been publishing in the *New Age*, she knew where to find it; and she provided *Rhythm* and its successor the *Blue Review* during 1912 and 1913 with a series of New Zealand stories: 'New Dresses' and 'The Little Girl', based on memories of her family; 'Ole Underwood' from her memory of a Wellington street character; 'The Woman at the Store', 'Millie', and 'How Pearl Button was Kidnapped' based on the Urewera notebook.

She began with the Urewera notebook. Murry received from her the story 'The Woman at the Store' and he printed it in his spring issue of 1912. So close is the dependence of one text on the other, she must have had the Urewera notebook open before her as she was writing 'The Woman at the Store'. The plot is simple: three travellers, one of them a girl, after riding over the plains, plan to set up their tent for the night by a lonely whare inhabited by a woman and her small daughter. The father is absent ('away shearing'). The child reveals, by a drawing, that the woman has murdered her husband. All the elements of the story and much of the language is derived directly from the Urewera notebook. The landscape is that covered twice by KM and her party on their camping trip, the great pumice plain between Rangitaiki and the Waipunga River. For the central characters, the woman and child, KM has combined two of her recorded impressions, her suspicions of marital discord at the Rangitaiki Hotel (see pp. 46 and 86) and the 'garrulous' woman with 'great boots' and the 'farm child' encountered the following evening (see p. 86). The setting is composite – KM has moved the Rangitaiki store a day's march to the east.

The language of the story follows closely the language of the notebook; sometimes it is identical. The 'heat' and the 'chuffing' horses, the 'shrilling' larks, the collocation of tussock and orchid and manuka, the rider's 'blue duck' trousers, the whare's 'horsehair sofa', the 'swampy creek', the absent man who is 'away shearing', the 'pair of dirty Bluchers', the narrator bathing in the creek, the boiling billy, all are in the notebook in virtually the same words. Whole phrases and incidents are transferred. The Rangitaiki hotel people in the notebook 'give us fresh bread'; in the story the woman offers to 'knock up a few extry scones'. The notebook's 'We are like children here all happiness' becomes in the story 'We behaved like two children . . . laughed and shouted to each other'. The violent thunderstorm of the notebook becomes, in the story, an integral part of the plot.

To Murry 'The Woman at the Store' was by far the best thing *Rhythm* had printed. The plotted story with a surprise ending was a form that KM rapidly grew out of; but it remains an effective piece of writing, its solid authenticity derived from KM's notes of 1907.

KM turned to the notebook once again later in the year, to write a quite different kind of story 'How Pearl Button was Kidnapped', which appeared in *Rhythm* in September 1912. This is a 'fairy story' with obvious allegorical overtones. Pearl is taken from her House of Boxes by two 'dark women' who mother her and she spends an idyllic day with 'other people of the same colour as they were' till she is discovered and returned to the House of Boxes. It is a reaction against the brittle sophistication of the *New Age*, a plea for warmth and simplicity. The flax basket of ferns, the rugs, the feather mats, the Maori interior are all derived from the notebook. KM is drawing on her notes on Umuroa and on Te Whaiti (where she had been presented with a 'Maori kit' or flax basket) and on her memories of the warm welcome the 1907 party had received from the Maori guide and his family. The following year KM provided Murry with one further 'backblock' story 'Millie', printed in June 1913 in *Rhythm*'s successor the *Blue Review*. It is a reworking of the violence of 'The Woman at the Store'. The landscape and setting are once more derived from the notebook.

With 'Millie' the Urewera notebook had exhausted its immediate usefulness and no further stories were directly based on her old camping record. The experience remained part of her. I do not think it accidental that when she came in 1922 to draw up her will, making sure that all would be left tidy behind her, the words that came to her were 'I desire to leave as few traces of my camping ground as possible'. For her it was no mere conventional turn of words.

I doubt if she opened the notebook after 1913. But phrases and images and incidents recorded there lay stored in her memory. 'At the Bay' is full of such memories. It opens with a single phrase – 'Very early morning'. 'Everyone' is asleep. Only the narrator is awake. This diary-like opening phrase and the ensuing collocation of bush/dew/snapping of twigs forms an image that finds its ultimate source in these early morning scenes (everyone but KM asleep) recorded several times in the notebook.

The day after the trip concluded, KM wrote a poem in the notebook: the theme was the fragility of the flowers of the manuka – and of human life. This poem, never revised and probably forgotten, is the buried source of the sixth section of 'At the Bay', where Linda is covered by the falling flowers of the manuka, symbols of everything that is 'wasted, wasted'. (A more detailed discussion can be found in the text.)

One image haunted her for years. In the opening pages of the notebook she recorded the felled and burnt-over bush seen through the train window – masses of charred logs 'like strange fantastic beasts'. She returned to the image several times. Among her papers there is an unrhymed poem, in which the masses of logs have become rocks – 'like some herd of shabby beasts'. She marked this sheet 'revise', and elsewhere in her papers there is a revision: the unrhymed poem has been rewritten as prose; the beasts, which had been 'fantastic' and then 'shabby', have now become 'shaggy'. Finally, in 1921, fourteen years after she first set down the phrase in the Urewera notebook, it all came right in the precise and meticulous imagery of 'At the Bay' – 'Over there on the weed-hung rocks that looked at low tide like shaggy beasts come down to the water to drink . . . .'.

Is it any wonder that the Urewera notebook survived? The *New Age* had cast its young writer in a single role, provider of brittle and 'bitter' sketches, firmly rejecting her attempts to break away from the formula that had been established for her.[44] Murry's quite casual invitation to write something different led her back to the notebook which she had brought with her from Wellington. In a few years it was going to lead to the great New Zealand stories of her maturity.

Note on the Text

KM headed her notebook 'K. Mansfield, 4 Fitzherbert Terrace, Wellington, N.Z.' and added the date 'November 1907'. The first entry is undated but is likely to be 15 November. KM wrote up her notebook daily, generally adding the date or the day of the week, but on occasion she wrote 'on the march' and these latter entries are difficult to decipher. Her pages are closely packed, with few paragraph divisions. An entry finishing mid-line is followed immediately by the next entry (even if the following entry was written the next day). In presenting the notebook I have preserved her text and her punctuation. But each of her entries is printed as a separate 'incident', to which I have added a head-note to supply narrative continuity and offer the necessary background information.

KM on occasion made a deletion and an alteration. Where these show evidence of deliberate stylistic revision (and not merely the immediate correction of an error) they have been preserved. My occasional editorial intrusion is indicated by square brackets. The editor and Mrs Margaret Scott made independent transcripts and then cross-checked. There are some readings where I am still uncertain, which may yet yield to a combination of insight and of luck. Unconfirmed readings are marked †. KM had a habit of entering casual jottings (not necessarily related to the text) in blank areas. These are gathered together and may be found in the appendix.

31

L. ROTORUA

L. Rotoiti

ROTORUA **11**

L. Tarawera

Waikato

Pareheru

Atiamuri

River

12

Waiotapu

10

Rangitaiki River

Troutbeck Stati
Galatea

6

Waikato
Riverside camp

13

Kaingaroa
Plains
camp

TAUPO

Huka Falls

14

5

Te Whaiti

7/9

LAKE
TAUPO

Umuroa

8

Ruatah

L. Waikaremoana

Rangitaiki
(Hotel, Store)

4

Roadman's Paddock,
Rununga

15

Waipunga Falls

Sketch map of

3/16

Tarawera

CAMPING TRIP
1907

*(camping sites numbered
in sequence)*

2/17

Te Pohue

Hawke
Bay

Eskdale

1/18

NAPIER

Hastings

CAPE KIDNAPPER

The Urewera Notebook

KM and Millie Parker set off by train from Wellington in mid-November 1907. Millie Parker, six years older than KM, was the daughter of a chemist and niece of Robert Parker, a well-known music teacher. Both young women played in duets and trios in Wellington. Millie Parker had secured for KM an invitation to join a camping trip, led by her relatives, the Ebbetts, of Hastings. She is the 'F. T.' ('fellow traveller') of the notebook.

They left Wellington by the morning (7.15 a.m.) train, which stopped at Kaitoke for morning tea about 9.0 a.m. and for lunch in the late afternoon at Woodville ('Jakesville'). They reached Hastings in the evening and stayed with Mr and Mrs Ebbett. George Ebbett, a Hastings solicitor, was an experienced camper, a Maori speaker, with a considerable knowledge of Maori history and ethnology, and a collector of Maori artifacts. Although he does not figure in the notebook, he was responsible for KM's references to Maori history and for her accurate knowledge of Maori place-names. The first entry describes the train journey. Since KM has included a pencil-sketch of Millie (sitting opposite her), this passage was probably written during the afternoon in the train._

On the journey the sea was most beautiful – a silver point etching and a pale sun breaking through pearl clouds – There is something inexpressibly charming to me in railway travelling – I lean out of the window – the breeze blows, buffeting and friendly against my face – and the child spirit – hidden away under a thousand and one grey City wrappings bursts its

33

bonds – and exults within me – I watch the long
succession of brown paddocks – beautiful with here a
thick spreading of buttercups – there a white
sweetness of arum lilies – And there are valleys – lit
with the swaying light of broom blossom – in the
distance – grey whares – two eyes and a mouth – with
a light petticoat frill of a garden – creeping round
them On a white road once a procession of patient
cattle – wended their way, funereal wise – and ~~afar~~
behind them a boy rode ~~past~~ on a brown horse
something in the poise of his figure in the strong
sunburnt colour of his naked legs reminded me of
Walt Whitman[1]   Everywhere on the hills – great
masses of charred logs – looking for all the world like
strange fantastic beasts a yawning crocodile, a
headless horse – a gigantic gosling – a watchdog – to
be smiled at and scorned in daylight – but a veritable
nightmare in the darkness – and now and again the
silver tree trunks like a skeleton army invade the hills
– At Kaitoki the train stopped for 'morning lunch' –
the inevitable tea of the New Zealander – The F.T.
and I paced the platform peered into the long wooden
saloon where a great counter was filled with ham
sandwiches and cups and saucers – soda cake and
great billys of milk – We did not want to eat – and
walked to the end of the platform – and looked into
the valley – Below us lay a shivering mass of white
native blossom – a little tree touched with scarlet – a
clump of toi-toi[2] waving in the wind – and looking

34

for all the world like a family of little girls drying their hair – Late in the afternoon we stopped at Jakesville – How we play inside the house while Life sits on the front door step and Death mounts guard at the back.

Early in the morning of Sunday 17 November 1907, the four other members of the party assembled at the Ebbett house – Mr Hill (a Hastings farmer), Ann Leithead (from a Hawke's Bay station), and a recently married couple, the Webbers. H. J. Webber was a Hastings chemist and KM soon became friendly with his wife, who was the closest to her in age of the party's members.

After breakfast at the Ebbetts', they left in two vehicles, each drawn by two horses, a roofed 'coach' (with open sides) with seating for four, and a luggage waggon, on which all took turns in travelling. The party travelled north and camped that evening at Petane in the Esk valley, sleeping (men and women on either side) in a large white framed tent divided by a central partition. The next entry was written on the morning of Monday 18 November.

After brief snatches of terribly unfreshing sleep I woke – and found the grey dawn slipping into the tent – I was hot and tired and full of discomfort – the frightful buzzing of the mosquitos – the slow breathing of the others seemed to weigh upon my brain for a moment and then I found that the air was alive with birds' song – From far and near they called and cried to each other – I got up and slipped through the little tent opening on to the wet grass – All round me the willow[3] still full of gloomy shades – the

Camp by the willows, Eskdale, Hawke's Bay.
Ann Leithead, Millie Parker, Mrs Ebbett, Mrs Webber, KM (back to
camera), Hill, Ebbett (loading luggage waggon). The party camped
here on the first and last nights of the trip, 17 November and
14 December, 1907.

caravan in the glade a ghost of itself – but across the clouded grey sky the first streak of rose colour – blazoned in the day – The grass was full of clover bloom I caught up my dressing gown with both hands and ran down to the river – and the water flowed on – musically laughing – and the green willows – suddenly stirred by the breath of the dawning day – sway softly together – Then I forgot the tent and was happy

A double row of dashes in the MS at this point indicates a change of scene. What follows in the notebook is a description of the previous evening. The camp had been set up near the site of an 1866 engagement between the British forces (led by Major Fraser) and a party of Maoris, in which most of the Maoris were killed. It is likely that KM had her information from listening to Ebbett.

So we crept again through that frightful wire fence – which every time seemed to grow tighter and tighter – And walked along the white – soft road – on one side the sky was filled with the sunset – vivid clear yellow – and bronze-green and that incredible cloud shade of thick mauve – Round us in the darkness the horses were moving softly with a most eerie sound – visions of long dead Maoris – of forgotten battles and vanished feuds – stirred in me – till I ran through the dark glade on to a bare hill – the track was very narrow and steep – and at the summit a little Maori whare was painted black against the wide sky – Before it – two cabbage trees stretched out phantom fingers – and a dog, watching me coming up the hill, barked madly – Then I saw the first star – very sweet and faint – in the yellow sky – and then another and another like little holes – like pinholes[4] And all round me in the gathering gloom the wood hens called to each other with monotonous persistence – they seemed to be lost and suffering – I reached the whare and a little Maori girl and three boys – s̶a̶w̶ sprang from nowhere – and waved and beckoned – at the door a beautiful old Maori woman sat cuddling a cat – She wore a white handkerchief round her black hair and wore a green and black cheque[5] rug wrapped round her body – Under the rug I caught a glimpse of a very b̶r̶i̶ pale blue print dress – worn native fashion the skirt over the bodice –

The party set off on the morning of Monday 18 November for Pohue, on the Napier-Taupo road. KM sat on the baggage in the luggage-waggon and wrote in her notebook the opening of a draft letter to her older sister Marie (Chaddie).

Petane Valley

Monday Morning
Bon jour – Marie dearest Your humble servant is seated on the very top of I know not how much luggage – so excuse the writing – This is a most extraordinary experience – Our journey was charming – A great many Maoris in the train – in fact I lunched next to a great brown fellow At Woodville

– that was a memorable meal – we were both starving
– with that dreadful silent hunger – Picture to yourself
a great barn of a place[6] – full of primly papered
chandeliers and long tables – decorated with paper
flowers – and humanity most painfully en évidence
you could cut the atmosphere with a knife –

*The draft letter breaks off, and is followed by a brief description of
the landscape on the way up the valley towards the long ascent to
Pohue.*

Then the rain fell heavily drearily – on to the river
and the flax swamp – then mile upon mile of dull
plain – In the distance – far and away in the distance
the mountains were ~~covered~~ hidden behind a thick
grey veil –

*The next entry is a 'diary' entry. The party spent the day travelling
the twenty-two miles to Pohue along the rough coach-road. They
made camp in the early evening. KM, Millie Parker and Mrs
Webber walked by a bush track to the Ohurakura station, visiting
the sheep sheds and the homestead. They returned to find the dinner
cooked and were met with 'black looks' from the others. At Pohue
KM posted letters to her family – her 'accounts' at the end of the
notebook shows that she had already sent them several telegrams.*

Monday – The manuka[7] and sheep country – very
steep and bare – yet relieved here and there by the
rivers and willows – and little bush ravines – It was
intensely hot – we were tired and in the evening
arrived at Pohui where Bodley has the accomodation

House – and his fourteen daughters grow peas – we camped on the top of a hill – mountains all round and in the evening walked in the bush – a beautiful daisy pied creek – ferns, tuis and we saw the sheep sheds – smell and sound – 12 Maoris – their hoarse crying – dinner cooking in the homestead – the roses – the Maori cook – Post letters there – see Maoris –

Webber believed in an early start. Next morning, Tuesday 19 November, he had his party up and 'working' by 5.0 a.m. It was to be a long day. There were twenty-four miles to be driven between Pohue and the next camp, at Tarawera. The road was rough and hilly, with spectacular bush and mountain scenery. The 1907 road (from which the modern swift motor highway deviates considerably) plunged for miles into several deep river valleys and climbed two mountain ranges, at Titiokura Saddle (2,289 feet) and at Turangakuma (2,625 feet). Ebbett took the precaution of securing a fifth horse at Pohue for the heavy luggage waggon, but the party spared the horses by walking the long steep uphill sections. KM at nineteen was a fit young woman – there must have been at least a dozen miles of walking called for and a total upwards climb on foot of between 2,000 and 3,000 feet. Her enjoyment of the whole day, with its concluding bathe in a hot mineral bath in the evening, is manifest.

Tuesday morning start very early – Titi-oKura – the rough road and glorious mountains and bush – The top of Taranga-kuma – rain in the morning – then a clear day – the view – mountains all round and the organ pipes[8] – we laugh with joy all day – we lunch past the Maori pah and get right into the bush – In the

afternoon more perfect bush and we camp at
Tarawera Mineral baths – the old man – the candle in
a tin – the scenery – the old shed – the hot water – the
feeling[9] – the road – How we sleep –

*Wednesday 20 November was, to begin with, similar to the
previous day – bush, rough mountain road, uphill walking. The
mountainous part of the route concluded at the Waipunga River,
where the party stopped for lunch and a view of the Waipunga Falls.
As they rested after lunch, KM wrote in the notebook a long draft
letter to her mother. In the afternoon they continued their
twenty-one miles day's journey. The road at this point enters open
pumice country, and KM was to use, some years later in 'The
Woman at the Store' her memories of the journey and the 'white
pumice dust swirled in our faces'. They camped that night at
Rangitaiki, where there was a hotel, a store, and a post office, where
KM posted letters to her family.*

Next day walking and bush – clematis and orchids –
meet Maori[10] by the ploughed field and at last come
the Waipunga falls – the fierce wind – the flax and
manuka – the bad roads – camp by the river[11] – and
then up hill – the heat to Rangitaiki Post letters –
camp on a peninsula – the purple – the ferns – the
clear long evening – the cream – the wild pigs –

*At this point in the notebook KM had originally written a ten-page
letter to her mother, sitting by the bank of the Waipunga River. She
tore the five pages from the notebook, intending to post them from
Rangitaiki. But – if she ever did send this letter – she must have
copied it out on better paper, since the detached five sheets were found
among her notebooks and papers on their arrival in Wellington after*

41

the 1957 sale. The Beauchamp family used telegrams frequently, and KM may have settled for a telegram – she records in her 'accounts' several sums for a 'wire'. The letter is now re-inserted (the torn edges match perfectly) at the point from which it was removed. It repeats – and expands – many details of the previous days' journeys, and the chatty style is in striking contrast to the conscious word-painting of the 'writer's notebook' which KM was keeping for her private use.

Waipunga Riverside
Wednesday

Dear my Mother –

I wrote you my last letter on Monday and posted it at Pohui in the afternoon – I continue my doings – We drove on through sheep country – to Pohui that night – past Maori pahs and nothing else – and pitched our camp at the top of a bare hill above the Pohui Accomodation House – kept by a certain Mr Bodley – a *great* pa-man[12] with 14 daughters who sit and shell peas all day! Below the hill there was a great valley – and the bush I cannot describe – It is the entrance to the Ahurakura Station – and though we were tired and hungry Millie, Mrs. Webber and I dived down a terrible track – and followed the bush – the tuis really sounded like rivers running – everywhere the trees hung wreathed with clematis and rata and miseltoe – It was very cool and we washed in a creek – the sides all smothered in daisies – the ferns everywhere – and eventually came to the homestead – It is a queer spot – ramshackle and

42

hideous – but the garden is gorgeous – A Maori girl –
with her hair in two long braids, sat at the doorstep –
shelling peas – and while we were talking to her – the
owner came and offered to show us the shearing
sheds – you think the sheep sound like a wave of the
sea – you can hardly hear yourself speak – He took us
through it all – they had only two white men
working – and the Maoris have a most strange bird
like call as they hustle the sheep – When we came
home it was quite dark and *how* I slept –

Next morning at five we were up and working –
and really looking back at yesterday I cannot believe
that I have not been to a progidious biograph show[13]
– We drove down the Titi-okura – and the road is one
series of turns – a great abyss each side of you – and
ruts so deep – that you rise three feet in the air –
scream and descend as though learning to trot – It
poured with rain early – but then the weather was
very clear and bright – with a fierce wind in the
mountains – We got great sprays of clematis – and
konini – and drove just through a bush path – But the
greatest sight I have seen was the view from the top
of Tarangakuma – You draw rein at the top of the
mountain and round you everywhere are other
mountains – bush covered – and far below in the
valley little Tarawera and a silver ribbon of river – I
could do nothing but laugh – it must have been the air
– and the danger – We reached the Tarawera Hotel in
the evening – and camped in a little bush hollow –

43

Grubby, my dear – I felt dreadful – my clothes were
white with dust – we had accomplished 8 miles of hill
climbing – so after dinner – (broad beans cooked over
a camp fire and tongue and cake and tea) we prowled
round an[d] found an 'aged aged man' with had the
key of the mineral baths – I wrapt clean clothes in my
towel – and then the old man rushed home to seize a
candle in a tin – he guides us through the bush track –
by the river – and my dear I've never met such a
cure[14] – I don't think he ever had possessed a tooth
and he never ceased talking – you know the effect?
The Bath House is a shed – three of us bathed in a
great pool – waist high – and we of course – in our
nakeds – The water was very hot – and like oil – most
delicious – We swam – I soaped and swam and soaked
and floated – and when we came out each drank a
great mug of dir mineral water – luke warm and
tasting like Miss Wood's eggs[15] at their worst stage –
But you feel – inwardly and outwardly – like velvet –
This morning we walked most of the journey and in
one place met a most fascinating Maori – an old
splendid man – he took Mrs Webber and me to see his
'wahine' – and child – It is a tropical day – the woman
squatted in front of the whare – she, too, was very
beautiful – strongly Maori – and when we had shaken
hands she unwrapped her offspring from under two
mats – and held it on her knee – The child wore a
little red frock and a tight bonnet – such a darling
thing – I wanted it for a doll – but in a perfect bath of

44

perspiration Mother couldn't speak a word of English and I had a great pantomime – Kathleen – pointing to her own teeth and then to the baby's – '*Ah*' Mother – very appreciative – '*Ai*' Kathleen – pointing to the baby's long curling eyelashes – '*Oh*' Mother – most delighted – '*Au*' And so on – I jumped the baby up and down in the air – and it crowed with laughter – and the Mother and Father – Leaving – shook hands with them again – Then we drove off – waving until out of sight – all the Maoris do that – Just before pulling up for lunch we came to the Waipunga Falls – my first experience of great waterfalls – they are indescribably beautiful – three – one beside the other – and a ravine of bush either side – The noise like thunder and the sun shone full on the water – I am sitting now on the bank of the river – just a few yards away – the water is flowing past – and the manuka flax and fern line the banks – Must go on – goodbye – dear – Tell Jeanne I saw families of wild pigs *and* horses here – and that we have five horses such dear old things – they nearly ate my head through the tent last night – I am still bitten and burnt – but oil of camphor, Solomon solution – glycerine and cucumber – rose water – are curing me – and I keep wrapt in a motor veil – This is *the* way to travel – it is so slow and so absolutely free and I am quite fond of all the people – they are ultra-Colonial but they are kind and good hearted and generous – and always more than good to me – We sleep tonight at the

Rangitaiki and then the plains and the back blocks –
Love to everybody. I am *very* happy –
Your daughter
Kathleen
Later Posting at country shed can't buy envelopes Had
wonderful dinner of tomatoes – Ah! he's given me an
hotel envelope –   K

*KM visited the Rangitaiki Hotel, meeting the landlord and his wife
and daughter. The following entry (expanded in a draft letter to her
mother – see Monday 25 November) indicates that KM felt herself
in the presence of some marital discord. It was this situation
(whether real or merely imagined), fitted out with different people
she met in a locale later in the journey, that was to become four years
later the double origin of her story 'The Woman at the Store'.*

Woman and daughter – the man – their happiness –
forgive Lord – I cant –

*On Thursday 21 November the party turned off the Taupo road and
headed north – probably on a compass-bearing – over empty country
to Galatea, some forty-five miles away. They spent the next two
days traversing the Kaingaroa Plains, in 1907 (before the advent of
forestry and cobalt) a vast derelict pumice tract covered with tussock
and manuka scrub, in which there were only occasional traces of a
rough road. They encountered a scrub fire; and Ebbett, from the
'coach', shot a couple of ducks which Webber had to swim to retrieve.
By nightfall they were utterly lost – 'bushed'. It rained violently,
the ducks were a 'badly cooked' failure, and they had a wet,
miserable camp and a night disturbed by a storm.*

Thursday the plain – rain – long threading – purple
mountains – river ducks – the clumps of broom –

46

wild horses – the great pumice fire – larks in the sun –
orchids, fluff on the manuka – strawberries – After a
time manuka and a tree or two – more horses – it
rains violently – the fearful road – No water – Night
in the tent – the rain – climbing to see where anything
is – the quivering air – the solitude – Early bed – the
strange sound – the utter back blocks – Fear as to
whether this was the rain – we close tent fast – the
kitchen – at night sat among our wet clothes –

*On Friday 22 November, after this wet camp, Ebbett had the whole
party (without waiting for breakfast) on the way by 6.0 a.m. The
route was defined only by an occasional rut on the scrub-covered
pumice and they often lost what track there was. But meeting a
group of Maoris they boiled the billy and found a route, emerging
from the Kaingaroa Plains to the fertile and settled Galatea district
in the Rangitaiki valley. They lunched by the Rangitaiki River
(KM calls it the Galatea River from the name of the nearby
township). After lunch she settled down to write a lively account of
the strenuous day – but broke it off in sudden alarm. There had been
no water for the horses on the pumice plains and the thirsty horses,
freed from the vehicles, made a bolt for the river.*

In the morning rain first is the chuffing sound of the
horses – we get up very early indeed – and at six
o'clock ready to start – the sun breaks through the
grey clouds   There is a little dainty wind – and a
wide fissure of blue sky – Wet boots – wet motor veil
– wet coat – the dew shining in the scrub – No
breakfast – We start – the road grows worse and
worse – we seem to pass through nothing but scrub

47

covered valleys – and then suddenly comes round the corner a piece of road – Great joy but the horses sink right into it – the traces are broken – it grows more and more hopeless – The weather breaks and rain pours down – We lose the track again and again – become rather hopeless when suddenly far ahead we see a man on a white horse – The men leave the trap and rush off. By and by through the track we meet two other men Maoris in dirty blue ducks – one can hardly speak English – They are surveyors – We stop – boil the billy and have tea and herrings – Oh! how good – Ahead the purple mountain – the thin wretched dogs – we talk to them – *thin* – we drive the horses off but there is no water – the dark people – their conversation – E ta – Haeremai te kai[16] – it is cold – the crackling fire of manuka – walking breast high through the manuka – Lily of the valley – the ti pore[17] we approach Galatea. We lunch by the Galatea River – there is an island in the centre and a great clump of trees – the water is very green and swift – I see a wonderful huge horsefly – the great heat of the sun and then the clouds roll up – 'Mother's little lamb – isn't 'e?' she said, tossing the baby up in the air – 'When 'e's asleep', cried the girl, bringing a clean pinafore and a little starched bib – 'Hold the horses or they'll make a bolt for the river' – my fright –

The next entry bears clear signs of having been written on the jolting waggon. It recounts the afternoon. While the men were rounding up the horses, KM and the women took shelter in a Maori house. On the road again, they turned south to visit the 'city' – it was a tiny township and KM notes it as Murupara – and then headed east by a long straight road to their camping place for the night.

Encounter one man surveyor on white horse – his conversation – raupo whare in distance – Picture – At the City gates we pull up and walk into the 'city'. There is a store – an Accomodation House – and a G.P.O. Mrs Prodgers is here with the baby – and the Englishmen – it is a lovely river – the Maori women are rather special – the Post boy – the children – an accident to the horses – very great – the Maori room – the cushions – Then a straight road in a sort of basin of stony mountains[18] – Far away in the distance a little cloud shines in the sunlight – Through the red gate there were waving fields a fresh flax swamp – the homestead in the distance – trees among clouds – a little field of sheep willow and cabbage trees and away in the distance the purple bush in the shadow – sheep in for shearing –

They had arrived at the homestead of the Troutbeck station, a large (c.22,000 acre) sheep run that had been established in the eighteen seventies. The run occupied fertile valley country but the homestead, situated on its southern corner, was only a few miles away from the Te Whaiti gorge, which is the gateway to the rugged Urewera country. For all her 6.0 a.m. start and a strenuous and eventful day, KM – while Mrs Ebbett cooked the dinner – wandered around, contemplating the gloomy ranges of the Urewera mountains, talking to Maori children, and met in Bella ('the very dusk incarnate') one of the figures she will incorporate into a literary exercise before the trip concludes.

49

Washing-up in camp, Troutbeck Station,
Galatea – 'a beautiful place with a little patch of bush'.
Ann Leithead, Hill, KM, Mrs Ebbett, Mrs Webber, Ebbett,
Webber, Millie Parker.

Here we drive in and ask for a paddock   Past the
shearing shed – past the homestead to a beautiful place
with a little patch of bush – tuis – magpies – cattle –
and water running through – But I think from bitter
experience that we shall be eaten with mosquitos –
Two Maori girls are washing – I go to talk with them
They are so utterly kids – While the dinner cooks I
walk away – and lean over a giant log. Before me a
perfect panorama of sunset – long sweet steel like
clouds – against the faint blue – the hills full of gloom
– a little river with a tree beside it is burnished silver –
like the sea – the sheep – and a weird passionate
abandon of birds – their † strange cries – the fanciful
shapes of the supple jacks – – – – Then the advent of
Bella – her charm in the dusk – the very dusk
incarnate – Her strange dress – her plaited hair and
shy swaying figure – The life they lead here –

51

On Saturday 23 November KM in the morning visited the Troutbeck Station shearing sheds and watched the bustling activity. The party then took the road that led south-east and drove into the heavily bushed and mountainous Urewera country. KM, seeing those great trees for the first time, made a special note of the characteristic 'matai' bush of the region. On the way, the party met a ranger, 'one of the Warbricks', who greeted them courteously and accompanied them to the Maori township ('pah') of Te Whaiti, which (with a police station, a government store, and a post office) was the tiny administrative centre of the Urewera region. Arthur Warbrick was a well-known guide in the Rotorua area. His brother Albert[19] lived near Te Whaiti and it is his house (KM calls it the 'guide's whare') which the party was to visit two days later.

At Te Whaiti they were now deep in the little-known Urewera country, the homeland of the Tuhoe people, the last of the Maoris to admit European penetration. No more than twelve years earlier, they had been threatening armed resistance to European road-survey parties. KM's sharp eye notes the contrast between the Edwardian 'parlour' of the Maori house they visited at Te Whaiti, decorously furnished with chiming clock and horsehair sofa, and the brightly dressed 'almost threatening looking' crowd outside the post office, followers of Rua (the Tuhoe prophet and opponent of the white man). KM's instinct for a situation was remarkable. The Te Whaiti district constable was on the point of setting out to Rua's camp to 'inspect his doings' – and ultimately to serve on him a summons for non-payment of his dog tax (Rua tore up the summons).[20] KM knew nothing of this. But she sensed the hostile atmosphere.

In the shearing sheds – the yellow dress with huia feathers[21] on the coat jacket with scarlet rata blossom – The speed – heat – new look of the sheep – Farewell – The road to Te Whaiti – Meet the guide – Wild

strawberries – the pink leaved ferns – Matai –
Lunched at a space in the bush cut through a tree –
and then by devious routes we came to the pah – It
was adorable – Just the collection of huts – the built
place for koumara and potato[22] – We visit first the
house – No English – then a charming little place –
roses and pinks in the garden – Through the doorway
the kettle and fire and bright tins – the woman – the
children – the pink dress and red sleeves and all the
background – How she stands gathering her pleats of
dress – she can say just 'yes' – Then we go into the
parlour – photos – a chiming clock – mats – kits[23] –
red table cloth – horse hair sofa – the child saying
'Nicely thank you' – the shy children – the Mother of
the poor baby thin and naked – the other bright
children – her splendid face and regal bearing – Then
at the gate of the P.O. a great bright coloured crowd
almost threatening looking – a follower of Rua with
long Fijian hair and side combs – a most beautiful girl
of 15 – she is married to a patriarch – her laughing
face – her hands playing with the children's hair – her
smile –

*Warbrick saw them safely across the Whirinaki River, and they set
up camp by a whare belonging to his family, a short distance beyond
Te Whaiti. Although it was early summer, it was cold at that
altitude, and they kept a fire going all night.*

across the bad river – the guide – the swimming dogs
– it flows on – he stands in the water a regal figure

then his *alright* and we are out – the absolute ease of his figure – so fearless – he speeded our parting journey – his voice is so good when he speaks – most correctly and yet enunciates each word. We see him last stopping to brush his horses near a mound of tutu – amazingly emerald in colour – the sun is fearfully hot – We camp by the guide's whare – the splendour of the night – the late fire – whole of night – Then the birds calling through the night –

On Sunday 24 November they made another early start. Ebbett planned to return to Te Whaiti the following night and in view of the steep road ahead lightened the load on the luggage waggon. KM knew she was 'on the way to Matatua' – it was Ebbett's intention to make his turning point at Mataatua, where there was a great carved Tuhoe wharepuni (meeting-house).

The route offers the most spectacular scenery in the North Island. In the ten miles after the camp at Te Whaiti the horses had to climb a high mountain road, descend a steep valley, climb again to the saddle of Tarapounamu to close on 3,000 feet, before descending to a branch of the Whakatane River, where at Umuroa Ebbett planned to camp. The valley contained the largest tract of flat land in the Urewera country and it was the ancestral settled area of the Tuhoe people. KM's reaction to the experience – 'gigantic and tragic . . . even in the bright sunlight so passionately secret' sounds like romantic exaggeration; but this vast, empty, mountain region of primaeval bush still overwhelms the traveller.

Sunday A splendid morning – washing in the creek – Leave early – leaving some luggage – on the way to Matatua the silver beech – the white flowers – that

54

Elysian valley of birds – the red tipped ferns – the
sound of the shot and then almost a bare hill among
green hills with bare tree trunks and a strong blue sky
– We meet a little flock of white sheep and a whare on
a hill – and called too – but no one is at home though
there is a suggestion of fire lately – From this saddle
we look across river upon river of green bush then
burnt bush russet colour – blue distance – and a wide
cloud flecked sky – All the people must doubtless
have gone shearing – I see no one – – – – Above the
whare there is a grave A green mound looking over
[*four words indecipherable*] the valley – the air – the
shining water – the sheep swift and terror-stricken flee
before us – once – at the head of a great valley the
blazing sun uplifts itself – like a gigantic torch to light
the bush – it is all so gigantic and tragic – and even in
the bright sunlight it is so passionately secret – And in
[*several words indecipherable*] look – We begin to reach
the valley – broad and green – red and brown
butterflies – the green place in vivid sunlight and the
silent and green bush – The sunlight slanting in to the
trees – an island – then a river arched with tree fern –
And always through the the bush the hushed sound of
water running on brown pebbles – It seems to breathe
the full deep bygone essence of it all – a fairy
formation of golden rings – then rounding a corner
we pass several little whares deserted – and grey –
they look very old and desolate – almost haunted – on
one door there is a horse collar and a torn and

55

scribbled notice – flowers in the garden – one clump of golden broom – one clump of yellow irises – Not even a dog greets us – all the whares look out upon the river and the valley and the bush gloried hills. These trees smothered in cream blossom –

Meeting a Maori girl on the road, KM dashed down a few brief sketch-notes. Later, when she had days of leisure at Taupo, she worked up these notes into a full-blown literary essay, which she called a vignette (see p. 83).

Blue skirt – great piece of greenstone – Black hair – white and red bone ear rings –

The party reached the flat ground where the valley opened out at Umuroa to find more whares 'deserted' (at this season the younger Tuhoe men and their families moved as far as Hawkes Bay to earn cash by shearing, leaving their animals to be tended by the old people). They set up their camp by the river.

We plunge back into the bush and finally reach a whare – several whares – deserted now but showing signs of recent habitation – A white cow and her calf are tethered to the side of the road a brown cow and her brown calf and a grey mare and a grey and brown leading a little foal are the sole inhabitants – there is a great open clearing here – and we decide to pitch the tent.

KM woke up on the morning of Monday 25 November in the camp by the riverside and recorded her impressions.

We are up Early – the wet bushes brush against my face – and sunflecked avenues – The new bracken is like H. G. Wells[24] dreaming flowers like strings of beads – the sky in the water like white swans in a blue mirror –

(The notebook from this point onwards shows a feature characteristic of most of her later notebooks – the sequence of the pages does not always indicate the order in which they were written. She has a habit of missing out some pages and writing a note (often a draft letter) some pages 'ahead', going back to fill the blank pages later. She will also backtrack to a verso left blank – its entry is thus later than what follows. On occasion, what follows of her text does not represent the sequence of the pages of the notebook but what an examination of the MS indicates was the sequence of the writing.)
On the Monday morning Ebbett led the men in the party to the finely carved wharepuni (meeting-house) built in 1890 for the Tuhoe leader Te Kooti. On the return from the eight-mile walk, the men reported the distance was too great for the women, and the whole party visited the 'great pah' at Ruatahuna, a mile and a half distant.

We lunch and begin to decide whether to go to the Wharepuni – the men folk go but eventually come back and say that the walk is too long – also the heat of the day but there is a great pah 1 ½ miles away – there we go – the first view – a man on the side of the road – in a white shirt and brown pants waits for us –

57

Opposite is a thick black Maori fence – in the distance across the paddock several whares clustered together like snails upon the green patch – And across the paddock a number of little boys come straggling along – from the age of twelve to three – out at elbow – bare footed – indescribably dirty – but some of them almost beautiful – none of them very strong – There is one great fellow I see – who speaks English – black curls[25] clustering round his broad brow – rest almost languor in his black eyes – a slouching walk and yet there slumbers in his face passion might and strength. Also a little chap –

From Umuroa the party returned to a camping site at Te Whaiti 'by the guide's whare' and there KM and some of her companions played string games ('nga maui') with the Maori children. But after Umuroa, Te Whaiti was a disappointment. Some years previously, a government store (under the charge of Elsdon Best) had been set up there as headquarters for the construction of the road to Ruatahuna. This had brought employment to the district, wages – and inevitable Europeanization. KM, having now met and been impressed by the 'primitive' Tuhoe people in their ancestral homeland, found in the anglicized Maoris of Te Whaiti 'nothing of interest'.

We play 'Nga maui'[26] with the Maori children – in the sunshine – Their talk and their queer droll ways – They laugh very much at us but we learn too – tho it is difficult and tedious, too, because our hands are so stiff – One girl is particularly interesting with auburn hair and black eyes – She laughs with an indescribable

The party returning to Te Whaiti
after visiting Ruatahuna, in the Urewera country.
Webber, with his wife beside him, drives the luggage waggon.
Ebbett leads, driving the 'coach'. Note the fifth horse, which Ebbett
secured at Te Pohue, before he tackled the main range on the
way to Tarawera and Rangitaiki.

manner and has very white teeth – Also another
Maori in a red and black striped flannel jacket – the
small boy is raggedly dressed in brown – his clothes
are torn in many places – he wears a brown felt hat
with a 'koe-koea'[27] feather placed rakishly to the side.
Here, too, I meet Prodgers – it is splended to see once
again real English people – I am so tired and sick of
the third rate article – Give me the Maori and the
tourist but nothing between – Also this place proved
utterly disappointing after Umuroa which was
fascinating in the extreme – The Maoris here know
some English and some Maori not like the other
natives – Also these people dress in almost English
clothes compared with the natives [t]here – and they
wear a great deal of ornament in Umuroa and strange
hair fashions – I found nothing of interest here –

*That evening she wrote (and then deleted) a few lines of a draft letter
to her mother. The theme was the situation at the hotel back in
Rangitaiki, which still concerned her.*

Monday

Well Mother I posted your letter at the Rangitaiki
Hotel – and on the way out I saw the land-lord's wife
– and thinking that she was a happy woman
questioned her as to her offspring

*That evening they visited the Warbricks. KM was fascinated by the
shy young niece, Johanna, returned from school to read Byron – and*

milk the cow. At the head of a page KM wrote her name in full 'Johanna Hill Warbrick' and beside it 'Longfellow'. Did the two young women discuss Longfellow? Or had KM promised a copy?

On Monday night we slept outside Warbrick's whare – rather sweet Mrs Warbrick is such a picture in her pink dressing gown – Her wide native hat her black fringe – her hands are like carving – She gives us a great loaf of bread – leans swaying against the wire fence – in the distance I see the niece Johanna watering her garden with a white enamel tea pot – She is a fat well made child with a blue pinafore her hair plaited and most strange eyes – Then she milks the cows – and Wahi brings us a great bowl of milk and a little cup of cream – Also a cup of lard – she dines with us – teaches me Maori and smokes a cigaret – Johanna is rather silent – reads Byron and Shakespeare and wants to go back to school – W [*Mrs Webber*] teaches her fancy work. At night we go and see her – the clean place – the pictures – the beds – Byron and the candle-like flowers in a glass – sweet – the paper and pens – photos of Maoris and Whites too – Johanna stays by the door We see her jewelery her clothes – I got a Maori kit. W [*Mrs Webber*] thinks the old people at Umuroa so dirty – yes – Would I like to sleep there? – hot water – home in the dark – Johanna more silent – there is something sad about it all – she is so lonely – Next day they see us off I hear –

Te Whaiti, in the Urewera country.
Standing: Webber, KM, Mrs Webber, Millie Parker,
Ann Leithead. Sitting: Mrs Ebbett, Ebbett (wearing Maori cloak),
with Te Whaiti Maoris. Standing beside Ann Leithead is
Alfred Warbrick, the guide from Rotorua, whose family had
property in the area. The Maori in the cloak is
probably his brother Albert.

Tuesday 26 November saw another early start. KM had time to visit another Maori family and take a sad farewell of Johanna. Five years later something of the warm welcome by this Maori family found its way into KM's story 'How Pearl Button was Kidnapped'.

the guide's horse going in the night – she [*KM*] has been up very early – J [*Johanna*] is shyer today – she [*KM*] talks to the little boy from over the road – Now the boy's Mother comes a worn but rather beautiful woman who smiles delightfully – Yes, she has five children tho she looks so young – and the girl is shearing now – It is in Winter that it is so cold – all snow – and they sit by the fire – never go out at all – just sit with many clothes on and smoke – Farewell – Johanna again waters the flowers – soon she will go to milk the cow – and then begin again – I suppose –

Leaving their camp at Te Whaiti, they drove once again over the Kaingaroa Plains, due west to the volcanic region. Their camp that night was to be at Waiotapu. On the easy road over the plains Ebbett for a time allowed KM to drive. They passed the shattered mountain Tarawera, which had erupted disastrously in 1886 – KM's instinctive admiration for Warbrick would have been even deeper had she known he had performed heroic rescues after that disaster.

So we journey from their whare to Waiotapu – a grey day and I drive – long dust-thick road and then before us Tarawera with the great white cleft – The poverty of the country – but the gorgeous blue mountain – all round is a great stretch of burnt manuka –

*Later KM wrote a full account of the wonders – and the weariness –
of the day. But she found the belching mud volcano of Waiotapu
'disgusting'. She went to bed, wet, weary, and sick with the fumes of
sulphur. She was not to recover for some days.*

On the journey to Waiotapu – In the distance these hills
– to the right almost violet – to the left grey with rain
– Behind a great mount of pewter colour and silver –
And then as we journey a little line of brilliant green
trees and a mound of yellow grass – We stop at a little
swamp to feed the horses – and there is only the
sound of a frog – Intense stillness – almost terrible –
Then the mountains are more pronounced – they are
still most beautiful and by and bye a little puff of
white steam – We pass the forest tree plantations and
by turns and twists the road pass several steam holes –
Perfect stillness – and a strange red tinge on the cliffs
– the baked red of the earth showing through – We
passed one oily bright green lake – round the sides the
manuka clambered in fantastic blossoming – The air is
heavy with sulphur – more steam – white and fine –
Camp by a great sheet of water here the frogs croak
dismally – it is a grey evening – Bye and bye we go to
see the mud volcano – marvellous – oh so different –
mount the steps – all slimy and grey – and peer in – It
bulges out of the bowl in great dollops of loathsome
colour – like a boiling filthy sore upon the earth and a
little boiling pool below a thin coating of petroleum –
black ridged – Rain began to fall – she is disgusted

and outraged – Coming back the horrible road the long long distance and finally soaking wetness and hunger – Bed – and wetness again –

On Wednesday 27 November the party left Waiotapu and drove some nineteen miles to Rotorua. On the way they climbed the Pareheru hill, from which there was a spectacular view. It was to be KM's only agreeable memory of Rotorua. Waiotapu's smell was followed by Rotorua's even more powerful one (a contemporary guidebook has to admit its 'disagreeable sulphurous smell'). The party was in Rotorua till the morning of Sunday 1 December, and for KM every hour was one of sick misery. She bathed in the Rachael and the Priest hot baths at the sanatorium; she went for a day-trip on the lake; she dutifully visited Whaka; she bought presents for the family in Wellington, and one for Mrs Webber's birthday. But she was sick and 'fearfully low'. The only bright spots were letters from the family, awaiting her at the local branch of the Bank of New Zealand (Harold Beauchamp, her father, was a director and had made the arrangement), and on the Saturday a chance meeting with T. E. Y. Seddon, M.P. ('Tom'), son of the late Prime Minister, and one of her Wellington escorts. He found her in tears and took her to lunch. Apart from Pareheru ('that little Hill'), Rotorua was a disaster, and the jumbled and repetitive entries tell their own story.

The morning is fine but hot – the nearer they get to the town the more she hates it – perhaps it is smell – it is pretty hot – a rise to see the Pareheru[28] – they pass Whaka[29] – ugly suburban houses – ugly streets old shaking buses – crowds of the veiled tourists – But letters are good – and they camp in a paddock behind

66

the puffing trains – how nice the old lady is next door
– and her flowers – her white piccotes and briar roses
– that evening she has a bath – Thursday the
loathsome trip – Friday so tired that she sits in the
sanatorium grounds all the morning and that evening
– horrid the purple bowl – I bought † presents in
Whaka – the [*indecipherable word*] good and the cerise
handbags – Also the little naked boys and girls but the
coy airs – bah! Rain again Saturday letters – far more
– and lunch with Tom[30] – and the quiet afternoon –
fearful rain – up to the ankles – the wet camp the fear
of having to move – she thinks Rotorua is loathsome
and likes only that little Hill –
Thursday on the lake – a beautiful day – the people –
Rotorua is not what I expect –
Friday – We spent day in the grounds – bathing and
walked afternoon – baths – Priest and Rachael – Feel
fearfully low – Saturday – Rain – letters – the hotel –
rain – and at night – Sunday leave   Fine day

*In Rotorua she replied to her family letters. She wrote to Marie
(Chaddie) but there is no draft in the notebook. There is, however,
the beginning of a letter to her mother, followed by a longer draft. To
her mother she put on a braver face. But a passing train interrupts
her writing.*

Rotorua   Friday
Mother dearest
    Thank you for your wire which I received today

and for Chaddie's lovely letter – so Vera has definitely left.[31] I can hardly realise it – What a strange household you must be feeling – You sound most gay at home – I am so glad – I wrote to Chaddie on Wednesday Yesterday was very hot indeed – A party of us went a Round Trip to the Hamurana Spring – the Ohere Falls, across Lake Rotoiti to Tikitere, and then back here by coach – I confess, frankly, that I hate going trips with a party of tourists – they spoil half my pleasure – don't they yours? You know one lady who is the wit of the day and is 'flirty', and the inevitable old man who becomes disgusted with everything, and the honeymoon couple – Rotorua is a happy hunting ground for these – We came back in the evening grey with dust – hair and eyes and clothing – so I went and soaked in the Rachael bath – the tub is very large – it is a wise plan to always use the public one – and there one meets one sex very much 'in their nakeds' – Women are so apt to become communicate on these occasions that I carefully avoid them – I came home – *dined*, and went into town with Mrs. Ebbett – We ended with a Priest Bath – another pleasant thing, but most curious – At first one feels attacked by by by Deepa's[32] friends – the humble worms – the bath is of aerated water, very hot, and you sit in the spring – but afterwards you   A train again – there is no † missing this affliction –

*The earlier (and firmly deleted) draft of the above letter makes the
hot baths rather less attractive — which may be why KM had offered
a more cheerful report.*

Rotorua   Friday
Mother dearest
    Thank you for your wire which I received today
and for Chaddie's lovely letter So Vera has definitely
gone I can hardly realise it What a strange household
you must be feeling As to me:– I have been bathing
twice a day – the Rachael and the Priest's Bath they
are delightful, but take it out of you to a very

*On Sunday 1 December the party made the usual early start and left
for the next camp-site, at Atiamuri, on the Waikato River, some
twenty-four miles away. She began with one distraught entry.*

Sunday
. . . I am tired to death with a headache and a
thoroughly weary feeling –

*Later, on the jolting waggon, she set down the stages of her recovery.
The smell of sulphur left behind, even Rotorua in retrospect was
'beautiful' and Whaka's vapours 'fanciful'.*

Sunday morning the early start it seems at each mile
post her heart leaps – But as they leave it the town is
very beautiful and Whaka full of white mist –
strangely fanciful she almost wishes – and – oh, it is
too hot where they lunch – she feels so ill – so tired –
her headache is most violent – she can hardly open her

69

eyes – but must lean back – each jolt of the cart pains her – but the further they go the load begins to lighten – they meet a Maori again – walking along barefooted and strong – she shouted Te nakohi[33]? – and Kathie's heart

Later in the day, as her youthful resilience reasserted itself, she made a draft of an efficient little business letter to the Rotorua manager of the Bank of New Zealand.

Sunday   Nowhere
Dear Mr Millar –

I have to thank you for keeping my none too small amount of correspondence – I went to the Bank yesterday afternoon – foolishly forgetting that it was closing day. Would you kindly address any letters that may arrive for me c/o Bank of New Zealand Hastings – I shall be there on Saturday – This paper is vile, but I am once more on the march –

Once more thank you
Sincerely yours
K. M. Beauchamp

She was now sufficiently herself to compose three little literary descriptive sketches: one a landscape (it is probably the Waiotapu camp-site), and two of Rotorua scenes. Rotorua already has taken on romantic overtones.

Like stones bright bare hills – the great basins – the hills – the wonderful green flax swamp and always

Dear M Millar

I have to thank you for keeping my name too small amount of correspondence — went to the Bank yesterday afternoon forgetting that it was closing day. Would you kindly address any letters that may arrive for me c/o Bank of New Zealand Wellington. Shall be there on Saturday. This letter is only to say I am able to make it on Monday.

Give my love to Marilyn

Sincerely yours

K M Beauchamp

these briars – bush on the distant hills – the fascinating valleys of toitoi swayed by the wind – Silence again, and a wind full of the loneliness and the sweetness of the wild place – Kathie in the morning in the manuka paddock saw the dew hanging from the blossom and leaves – put it to her lips and it seemed to poison her with the longing for the sweet wildness of the plains – for the silent speech of the Silent Places – the golden sea of blossom –

Rotorua The first evening – the yellow sky – she lies on the grass tired – and hears the church[34] bell – It sounds across the darkness beautifully tender and touching like the touch of a child's hand in the dark – *The Hamurana Spring* – the still rain – the wonderful tangle of willow and rose and thorn – like Millais' Ophelia[35] – the undergrowth – and then the spring – like Maurice Maeterlinck[36] –

In the evening they were camped at Atiamuri. Next day KM wrote up a full account, the arrival at the hotel, the great towering rock above the river (Ebbett told her its history as a fighting pa), the rapids of the Waikato, which the women walked to view in the evening. KM envisages them as Wagnerian Rhine Maidens. KM is now firmly in control of her material.

Monday All Sunday the further she went from Rotorua the happier she became – Towards evening they came to a great mountain Pohataroa – it was very rugged and old and grim – an ancient fighting pah – Here the Maoris had fought – and at the top of

72

this peak a spring bubbled – In the blue evening it was
grim – forbidden silent – towering against the sky –
an everlasting monument – then rounding a corner
they saw the Waikato river – turbulent madly rushing
below them – and in a little hollow – girt about with
pine and willow tree the Atiamuri Hotel – As they
neared the house the persistent barking of dogs – the
people hanging over the fence – the old sedately
ridiculous turkeys – They camp in a paddock by the
river a wonderful spot – On one side the river on the
opposite bank great scrub covered mountains –
Before them a wide sheet of swift smooth water – and
a poplar tree – and a long straight [†] guardian of pines
– the willow tree – shaggy and laden – dips lazily
branches in the water – Just there the bank ahead of
them a manuka tree in full flowers leans towards the
water – the paddock is full of manuka – two grey
horses are outlined against the sky – After dinner –
they are hungry and tired – the man comes from the
hotel – Yes there are rapids to be seen and a good
track – they are not very far – she is gloomy and
fidgety – they start – go through the gates – always
there is a thundering sound from afar off – down the
sandy path – and they branch off into a little pine
avenue – the ground is red brown with needles – great
boulders come in their path – the manuka has grown
over the path – With head bent – hands out – they
battle through – Then suddenly a clearing of burnt
manuka – and they both cry aloud – There is the river

– savage, grey, fierce rushing tumbling – madly sucking the life from the still placid flow of water behind – like waves of the sea like fierce wolves – the noise is like thunder – right before them the lonely mountain outlined against a vivid orange sky – The colour is so intense that it is reflected in their faces, in their hair – the very rock on which they climb is hot with the colour – They climb higher – the sunset changes – becomes mauve – and in the waning light all the stretch of burnt manuka is like a thin mauve mist around them – A bird – large and widely silent – flies from the river right into the flowering sky – There is no other sound except the voice of the passionate river – They climb on to a great black rock and sit huddled up there alone – fiercely almost brutally thinking – like Wagner[37] – Behind them the sky was faintly heliotrope – and then suddenly from behind a cloud a little silver moon shone through – One sudden exquisite note in the night terza[38] The sky changed – glowed again and the river sounded more thundering – more deafening – They walked back slowly – lost the way – and found it – took up a handful of pine needles and smelt it greedily – and there in the distant paddock the tent shone like a golden poppy – waiting outside – the stars – and the utter spell – magic Mist moving – mist over the whole world – Lying – her arms over her head – she can see faintly like a grey thought the river and the mist – they are hardly distinct – She is not tired now – only happy –

Her recovery was accomplished. After a night's sleep, she wrote an ecstatic picture of dawn and sunrise beside the Waikato.

Goes to the door of the tent – all is very grey – there is no sun first thing – she can see the poplar tree mirrored in the water – The grass is wet – there is the familiar sound of crickets – As she brushes her hair a wave of cold air strikes her – lays cold fingers about her heart – it is the shadow from Pohataroa – the sun comes – the poplar is green now – the dew shines on everything – a little flock of geese and goslings float across the river – the mist feather white – rises from the mountain ahead – there are the pines – and there just on the bank the flowering manuka is a riot of white colour against the blue water – a lark sings – the water bubbles – she can just see ahead the gleam of the rapids – The mist seems rising and falling here comes that heron again for the last time – and now the day fully enters with a duet for two oboes – you *hear* it – Sunshine had there ever been such sunshine – they walked down the wet road through the pine trees – the sun gleamed golden – locusts crunched in the bushes – through her thin blouse she felt it scorching her skin and was glad –

On Monday 2 December, the relentless Ebbett left the Atiamuri camp and drove his party to the thermal area of Orakei Korako. The road was rough and primitive. He shot rabbits for supper and before they made camp that night they had seen the Aratiatia rapids of the Waikato. They camped on a flat between the Aratiatia Rapids and the Huka Falls, the thunder of which could be heard as they lay in the tent that night. KM wrote it all up that evening.

Monday   on the road to Orakei Korako – The rainbow Falls in a great basin – We mount the hill – at the summit we look down at mile on mile of brown river winding in and out among the mountains – the banks quivered with toi toi – All the plains for miles are like a mirror for the sky We climb to a great height – Then there came rapids – great foaming rushing torrents – they tore down among the mountains – thundering roaring – we drew rein – and there was a wide space of blue forget-me-nots – The quiet bush – and mist is on the golden moss – the silent river – the ducks – the mist – the quiet and there through the leaves and trees the water – Then the climb – the rocks – the uncertain foot walk – higher and higher – clinging to the trees – the shrubs till at last on the grey rock we fling ourselves – blue as the tropical sea where the rapids commence and then a tumultuous – foaming torrent of water leaping crashing snow white – like lions fighting – thundering against the green land – and the land stretches out ineffectual arms to hold it back – It seems there is nothing in the world but this shattering sound of water – it casts into the air a shower of silver spray –

76

The Aratiatia Rapids, Waikato River.
Ann Leithead, Millie Parker, Mrs Webber, KM, Webber.

it is one gigantic battle. I watch it and am thrilled –
then through more bush – the ferns are almost too
exquisite – gloomy shade – sequestered deeps – and
out again – another rock to climb – another view –
here the colouring is far more intense – the purple –
the blue – and the great green-lashed rock – the water
thunders down – foam rushes – then pours itself
through a narrow passage – and comes out in a wide
blue bay – And floating on the water are the [two
words indecipherable] – more rushing white – wider
passage – more eddies – and at last far in the distance
– a wide strong stretch of shadowed sweetness – *Peace*
– We plunge back again – there is a last view – very
near the water the sound is far louder and under it all I
hear the falls –

*In camp that night, haunted by the sound of the river, she wrote the
openings of two draft letters, one to Marie (Chaddie) and the other
to her 'baby' sister Jeanne.*

Monday Night

Dear Marie
I am a vagrant a Wanderer, a Gypsy tonight –
booming sound – it rises half a tone about each
minute but that is all – it never ceases – and when the
water catches the light there is a rainbow pink blue
white – But time is all too short –

In Bed   Monday Night

Dearest Baby

This will, I think be my last letter to you – before I reach home – I wrote last to Chaddie from Rotorua – I must say I hated that town – it did not suit me at all. I never felt so ill and depressed – It was, I

Tuesday 3 December was an equally strenuous day. They explored the Wairakei Geyser Valley in the morning and in the afternoon drove through the bush to the Huka Falls. Determined to miss nothing KM descended with the others down a series of wooden ladders and rough steps to emerge underneath the Falls. ('The descent', reads a contemporary guide-book 'is difficult, and the return much more so. None should attempt it without a guide.') This perilous expedition (long abandoned as a tourist attraction) KM simply took in her stride. Her stamina as a young woman runs counter to the popular notion of her.

Round a bend of the road and the river – we see poplars – tall and strong and a suggestion of a fence – Then more poplars – and then in the distance – a great patch of flowering potatoes mauve blue and white – There is no sign of people – not the sound of a dog – but we hear from among the manuka the deathlike thudding like a paddle wheel We go down to the dragon's Mouth[39] – it is a most difficult walk down a scrambling path – holding on by bushes and trees – then there is one fierce jump and we are there. It belches filthy steam and smoke – there is green slime and yellow scale like appearance infinitely impressive

79

– and always that terrible thudding engine like sound
– We walk on a broad flat terrace and there is so thin a
crust that one would have thought it almost
dangerous to move – we see a very small geyser and
the rock and mud and sulphur holes – Across the road
and in the manuka is the pink mud pool – the other
side of the river are many steam holes and signs
where geysers have been – And signs where terraces
might be – it is too brazenly hot for words – we hear
the whole time the noise –

Tuesday   We drive through Weiraki through the hot
day to the Huka high Falls – here the river is the
colour turquoise (peacock blue) the falls utterly
superb – frothing and foaming – the foam drops for a
long way down the water – again that sound – great
poplars at the side – in the distance the gleaming river
– But I was not so impressed at first sight – We drove
into the bush – then got on to a bridge – stood there –
and went quiet – all the shuddering wonder was
below us – In the afternoon we climbed down the
bank – first a ladder then rough steps – another ladder
– catching swaying laughing – bush to the side – and a
fern grotto – pale green – like Tannhauser[40] – green
ferns hang from the top all round in dampness and
beauty and we are below the falls – the mountain of
water the sound – the essence of it a peculiar green –
So we drove –

*Though the remainder of the route of the party is easy to follow –
Taupo and then by the Taupo–Napier road back to Hastings – the
timetable is problematic, because the evidence is conflicting. When
KM wrote her Rotorua banker on Sunday 1 December she told him
she would be in Hastings 'on Saturday' (7 December). The accounts
given by other members of the party (many years after the trip, one of
them fifty years later) cannot be reconciled. Ann Leithead and the
Webbers had different memories of the length of the trip (varying
from three to six weeks). Even the two Webber accounts (written
some years apart) do not agree with each other. Memory is a fickle
thing. KM's notebook is the only account which was kept day by
day, and her dating is demonstrably accurate and precise. Her last
Taupo entry has the figure '10' against it; and later in the Notebook
she notes that the camp on 14 December (clearly back at Petane in
the Esk valley) was 'the last night'. This suggests that the party
spent a full week at Taupo, leaving for the final stretch of the
journey on Wednesday 11 December. The men were equipped for
hunting and fishing; and the women clearly enjoyed their Taupo
camp site with easy access to hot mineral baths. They had done a
strenuous tour.*

*From the Huka Falls they drove 'over the hills' to Taupo on
Tuesday 3 December and set up camp in the grounds of the Terraces
Hotel. KM records her first impression of the Lake, its island
Motutaiko, and the great mountains of the Tongariro group.*

We come over the hills to Taupo – Before us the lake
– in the foreground blue, then purple – then silver –
on this side the pines – the gum trees – the clustering
houses – and a fringed yellow meadow – In the lake
the little Motutaiko – and beyond that clear water
mountains until at last Ruapehu snow covered
majestic – lord of it all – towers against the steel sky

81

clearly – behind us Tohara is under a cloud – all the
clouds are so vivid white – grey blue – On one side
there is a little jutting promontory of green flat land In
the † track the broom – We approach Taupo across a
white bridge – the peacock blue river   along a white
road – to the Lake Hotel – there are the Maoris
lounging in the sun one in a black and white blazer –
blue pants – In the shade an old Maori drunk – a little
child is crouched – soon other Maoris come out – help
the old man into a ramshackle cart where a white
boney horse is very lamed – The child cries and cries –
the old man sways to and fro – she holds on to him
with a most pathetic gesture – they drive out of
sight –

*The camp near the Terraces Hotel proved to be an ideal spot, and
KM finished the day 'blissfully happy'.*

Taupo
The road winds by the lake – then we mount through
great avenues of pines and acacias to the Terraces
Hotel – Here are lawns and cut trees – little corners
long hidden walks – shady paths – all the red brown
pine needle carpet – the house is not pretty but
poppies grow round it – All is harmonious and
peaceful and delicious – we camp in a pine forest –
beautiful – there are chickens cheeping – the people
are so utterly benevolent – We are like children here
all happiness – We dine – then the sunset then supper

82

at the Hotel – and the night is utterly perfect – we go
to the mineral baths – the walk there down the hill is
divine – the suggestion of running water – and
cypresses – it is very steep – And a fine bath though
very hot and a douche – so pleasant – Then home
tired – hot – happy – blissfully happy – We sleep in
the tent – the wind is our lullaby –

*Up to this point the party had been regularly up in the morning at an
early hour and had usually driven more then twenty miles each day.
The only break had been at Rotorua, and there KM was too sick to
write coherently. The break at Taupo gave her the time to write a
full-blown 'Vignette', the literary genre (if it can be called that)
which had provided her first publications in the Australian journal
the* Native Companion *in October and November. The Oscar
Wilde overtones of her published 'Vignettes' were now forgotten. In
Taupo, she wrote a very different 'Vignette', based on the lake and
mountain landscape and the Maoris she had been meeting, her
'heroine' a fusion of Johanna Warbrick and Bella, who had been 'the
very dusk incarnate' at Murupara, and – of course – of herself. For
the heroine's costume she used her notebook sketch written earlier at
Umuroa (see p. 56).*

VIGNETTE

Sunset Tuesday
I stand in the manuka scrub – the fairy blossom –
Away ahead the pines black – the soughing of the
wind – On my right the lake is cold, grey, steel-like –
the quiet land sleeps beside it – Away ahead in the
silver sea lies the island – then the wild sky –

83

everywhere the golden broom tossed its golden
fragrant plumes into the evening air – I am on a little
rise – On my right a great tree of mimosa laden with
blossom bends and foams in the breeze –

And, before, the lake is drowned in the sunset –
The distant mountains are silver blue – and the sky –
first † turns rose – then spreads into a pale ~~brown
colour~~ amber – Far away on my left the land is
heavily heliotrope – curving and sharply outlined –
and fold upon fold of grey sky – And far far ahead ~~in
the blue sky~~ – a ~~silver~~ little golden moon daintily
graciously dances in the blue floor of the sky – A
white moth flutters past me I hear always the
whispering of the water – I am alone – I am hidden
Life seems to have passed away drifted – drifted miles
and worlds so beyond this fairy sight –
Very faint and clear the bird calls – and cries – and
another on a little scarlet touched pine tree – close by
me – answers – with an ecstasy of song – then I hear
steps ~~coming~~ approaching – A young Maori girl
climbs slowly up the hill and she does not see me – I
do not move – She reaches a little knoll and suddenly
sits down native fashion her legs crossed [under her][41]
her hands clasped in her lap – She is dressed in a blue
skirt and white soft blouse – Round her neck is a piece
of twisted flax and around a long piece of greenstone
– is suspended from it – Her black hair is twisted
softly at her neck – she wears long white and red bone
earrings – She is very young – ~~she has~~ She sits – silent

– utterly motionless – her head thrust back – All the lines of her face are passionate violent – crudely savage – but in her lifted eyes slumbers a tragic illimitable peace – The sky changes – after the calm is all grey mist – the island in heavy shadow – silence broods among the trees – ~~the birds are silent now~~ The girl does not move But ~~ahead far far away~~ very faint and sweet and beautiful – a star twinkles in the sky – She is the very incarnation of evening – and lo – the first star shines in her eyes.

Taupo. December 1907

On the morning of Wednesday 11 December the party was up early. There was time for a final hot mineral bath before driving off.

We wake early – and wash and dress – and go into the bath again – Honeysuckle roses pinks & white periwinkles syringas and red hot pokers – those *yellow flowers* – The ground is sunflecked – Fruit trees with promise of harvest – the hot lake and pools – even the homely clothes prop – the lush grass – and more mimosa – the birds are magical – I feel I cannot leave but pluck the honeysuckle – and the splashes of light lie in the pine wood –

They set off for the final four days of the trip. After a brief stop at Opepe (scene of an engagement between British troops and Maoris in 1869, the details doubtless provided by Ebbett), they lunched at Rangitaiki. The hotel provided fresh bread but otherwise offered a cool welcome. The domestic situation seemed still unsettled. Then

85

they drove over the pumice road over the great Rununga plain and camped for the night beside a roadman's cottage. The roadman's wife greeted them (as recorded by Mrs Webber) with the words 'Come in and doss for a bit. I haven't got my drorin' room boots on', a phrase which KM kept repeating for the rest of the trip. This scene – the hot dusty pumice road over the plains and the meeting with the woman in boots – is one source of the story 'The Woman at the Store'. The details of the store – and the marital discord – come from Rangitaiki. There is a close verbal correspondence between the story and the 1907 Notebook.

Then goodbye Taupo and here are more plains – I feel quite at home again and at last we come to Opipi – the scene of a most horrible massacre – only 2 men were saved – one rushed through the bush – one was cutting wood – We stop to look for water and there are 2 men – the older the most perfect Maori like image the other pink shirt pink eyes – his horrible beard rolls his cigaret – Then we are in a valley of broom – such colour – it is strewn everywhere – I have never dreamed of so much blossom – then lunch at Rangitaiki – the store is so ugly – they do not seem glad or surprised to see us – give us fresh bread – all surly and familiar – and they seem troubled – And again the plain – We say goodbye to † Rangitaiki and a night fall coming the way – reach our camp – It is a threatening evening – the farm child – the woman her great boots – she has been digging – How glad she is to see us – her garrulous ways the child's thoughtful fascination – Then at night among the tussocks –

86

*Camp by the Waiarua stream, in paddock
below the house of 'Mr Himing, settler and roadman', Rununga.
The position of the luggage waggon and 'coach' indicates that the party
have driven from Rangitaiki over the pumice plain (left, beyond photo).
KM in 1911 used the ride over the pumice plain, the paddock and the
Himing house as the scene of 'The Woman at the Store'. The elevated
house-site was bulldozed flat during the construction and re-alignment of
the modern motor-road, but the energetic walker can still find the
camp-site, between the stream and the surviving traces
of the old pumice coach-road.*

On Thursday 12 December the party set off towards the Waipunga Falls, repeating in reverse the outward journey. KM makes no record of the camp sites for the 12th and 13th, in all probability their previous stopping-places at Tarewera and Pohue. The final camp among the willows on 14 December is clearly at Petane in the Esk Valley, and the party was back in Hastings on the 15th.

Then to the Waipunga falls – river – and rain follows – found a cover tarpaulin here a better shelter[42] – you fling on your clothes – bathe face and neck and back in a bucket of water – Then to the full glory of the morning – the dew on the grass and warrata – a lark thrilling madly – drinking a great pannikin of tea and a whole round of bread and jam – December 14th – the last night. Oh what a storm last night – And the coming of dawn – with the willows lashing together.

In Hastings that evening KM, her mind full of a memory of falling manuka blossom, saw in it the theme of a poem.

YOUTH

O Flower of Youth!
See in my hand I hold
This blossom flaming yellow and pale gold
And all its petals ~~scatter~~ flutter at my feet
Can Death be sweet?

Look at it now!
Just the pale green is heart
Heart of the flower seems white and bare
The silken wrapping scattered on the ground
What have I found?

If one had come
On a sweet summer day
Breathless, half waking – full of youth I say
If one had come it
What happens then?

Sighing it dies
In the dawn flush of life
Never to know the terror and the strife
Which kills all summer blossoms when they blow
Far better so
Ah! better better so

K. Mansfield   December 15th 1907

These romantic verses do not appear among her published poems. But the image (and the symbolism) of the falling yellow petals of the manuka remained in her memory and fourteen years later provided the opening of Section VI of 'At the Bay' – Linda in the garden under a manuka tree, covered with tiny yellowish flowers with a 'tiny tongue in the centre'. 'But as soon as they flowered, they fell and were scattered . . . all these things that are wasted, wasted'. KM hoarded her images, as she hoarded her papers.

The following day, 16 December, KM paid a visit to Napier, where EKB, with whom she had been involved in a passionate relationship earlier in the year, was staying. KM entertained EKB with *'excellent mimicries' of her travelling companions and of fat old Maori women. EKB found KM quite changed. KM had opened the Urewera notebook with a quotation from Oscar Wilde. EKB noted that the 'decadence' (she was thinking particularly of KM's literary poses with 'incense burning in her room') was gone – 'she had come down to earth violently'.*[44] *It was a very self-possessed KM who returned to Hastings to note down a list of things to be done in Wellington – 'Baby' (her sister Jeanne) and 'Albert Mallinson' to be seen, and 'send for my camera'. She set down firmly her work programme for the days ahead.*

> Timetable
> 6 – 8 technique
> 9 – 1 practice
> 2 – 5 write
> Freedom

Next morning, 17 December, a very poised and secure young woman (plans for the future well organized) took the train to Wellington.

In the train – December 17th – Has there ever been a hotter day – the land is parched – golden with the heat – The sheep are sheltering in the shadow of the rocks – in the distance the hills are shimmering in the heat – M. and I sitting opposite each other – I look *perfectly charming*.

Appendix

The Casual Jottings

KM used the Urewera notebook (as she used many of her later notebooks) as a repository for casual jottings. They do not form part of the 'narrative' and so I relegate them to an appendix. KM, I think, would have approved of their inclusion. *Journal*, 1954, p.210, indicates her attitude. She copies there a comment from W. Knight's Introduction to his edition of Dorothy Wordsworth's *Journal*:

All the Journals contain numerous trivial details . . . of the Wordsworth household – and, in this edition, samples of those details are given – but there is no need to record all the cases in which the sister wrote, 'Today I mended William's shirts' or 'William gathered sticks', or 'I went in search of eggs', etc. etc.

Since KM's comment on this passage was 'There is! Fool!', I feel encouraged to salvage all that is recoverable from the jottings, even including the proverbial laundry-list. I gather them together under convenient headings.

1. Quotations. The first sheet of the notebook opens with a quotation from Oscar Wilde:

A woman never ever knows when the curtain has fallen. O.W.

2. Place-names. Names (especially Maori) occur at the heads of pages. These names seldom apply to the specific page they head. KM used her top blank margins for *aide-mémoires*. Names occur as follows:

Urewera; Kaingaroa Plains; Petane Valley; Murupara; Galatea; Kaitoke; Rotorua; Orakei Korako; Aratiatia Rapids; Waitapu; Waiotapu; Taupo.

3. The following personal names appear:

Baby [sister Jeanne]; Albert Mallinson; Leslie Heron Beauchamp.

KM has underlined *Heron*; and the name of her brother is written two pages after the appearance of the heron over the Waikato River at Atiamuri. It is probably the starting point for the 'heron' image – 'heron' the equivalent of ideal happiness – which haunted her all her life.

4. A laundry-list (mid-journey, probably Rotorua):

1 nightgown; 3 petticoat bodices; 2 pr. drawers; dress shields; handkerchiefs; 2 pr. stockings; 3 vests; 2 blouses.

5. Maori words and phrases. KM uses in the text, without feeling any need of translation, the following words from the New Zealander's common stock of Maori:

matai (tree-name); toi-toi, manuka, raupo, tutu, rata, konini (plant-names); kumara (sweet potato); koe-koea, huia, tui (bird-names); nga maui (string games); whare (house); tena koe ('greetings'); wahine (woman, wife); pa, pah (village or fortified hill-village).

Twice she incorporates (without translation) Maori dialogue phrases into her narrative. In addition, she has several lists of Maori words with her English meanings. These are gathered together (in her spelling) as follows:

enohora – a goodbye to you who are staying
haerera – goodbye to you leaving
tamaiti – child
tangata – man
raupo – flax

92

e ta haeremai te kai – I say come to eat
Hau Hau pai marere – peace and goodwill
pipi wharuroa – a bird of good tidings and good news. Size of a
  skylark. It has a green striped head [the Shining Cuckoo].
te hoiho – the horse
te hipi – the sheep
te rori – the road
korero pakeha iakoi – do you speak English
rangi te wera – hot day
te rangi pai – fine day
kaha – strong
rewai – potatoes
In this part of the island [Urewera] 'wh' is 'f' –
  Te Whaiti = tə fɑi:tə
Waitapu – sacred water
wai raki – hot water
Wairakei – steaming water
hiko rere – blouse
pare kote – shirt
te putu – boots
potai – hat
te ata – breakfast
te awatea – dinner

6. A recipe.

¼ lb flour
¼ lb sugar
¼ lb walnuts
2 eggs
1 teaspoon baking powder
¼ lb butter
Bake in a moderate oven for about 20 minutes
– Mrs Webber

93

7. Accounts. As with many of her notebooks, the final two pages of the Urewera notebook are reserved for KM's accounts. She began by itemizing each piece of expenditure – one can identify her cup of tea at Kaitoke railway station and her lunch in the crowded Woodville station refreshment room on the first day, and the first two telegrams she sent back to Wellington.

She then decides to cease itemizing, copies out her first days' expenses and simply adds the cost of each new item. The whole trip cost her (on *her* reckoning) in out-of-pocket expenses £1-17-7½:

Tea		3
Lunch	2	0
		6
milk	1	0
wire		6
wire		7½
		3
	2	0
		6
	1	0
		6
		7½
		6½
	12	0
	1	6
	1	3
	1	6
	1	0
		9
	1	0
		7½
	3	9
	3	4
	2	0
	3	0
		2
£1	17	7½

$\mathcal{N}otes$

I (Introduction)

---

1. All writers on Katherine Mansfield face the purely technical problem of what to call her. The constant repetition of 'Katherine Mansfield' becomes somewhat long-winded. The 'Miss Mansfield' or the 'Mansfield' of some writers carries misleading connotations. In my *Undiscovered Country* (London, 1974), I called her 'Katherine', which one reviewer found too paternal. I have settled here for 'KM', a form she frequently used in her manuscripts.

2. KM to A. E. Rice, printed in *Adam International Review*, London, no.300, p. 93.

3. R. E. Mantz (and J. Middleton Murry), *The Life of Katherine Mansfield*, London, 1933; S. Berkman, *Katherine Mansfield*, New Haven, 1951; A. Alpers, *Katherine Mansfield A Biography*, New York, 1953.

4. *Journal of Katherine Mansfield*, 1927; *Journal of Katherine Mansfield*, Definitive Edition, 1954; *The Letters of Katherine Mansfield*, 2 vols., 1928; *The Scrapbook of Katherine Mansfield*, 1939; *Letters to John Middleton Murry*, 1951. All volumes were published in London and edited by John Middleton Murry.

5. KM to Vera. Turnbull MS.

6. *Journal*, 1954, p. 96.

7. *Letters*, 1928, vol. ii, p. 96.

8. Murry's treatment of KM's papers has been analysed in some detail in: Ian A. Gordon, 'The Editing of Katherine Mansfield's Journal and Scrapbook', *Landfall*, Christchurch, New Zealand,

March 1959, pp. 62-9; Philip Waldron 'Katherine Mansfield's Journal', *Twentieth Century Literature*, Hempstead, N.Y., January 1974, pp. 11-18.

9. *Journal*, 1927, Introduction by John Middleton Murry, p. xv.

10. *Carrington: Letters and Extracts from her Diaries*, ed. D. Garnett, London, 1970, p. 41.

11. Virginia Woolf to Vanessa Bell, 11 February 1917: *The Question of Things Happening, The Letters of Virginia Woolf*, London, 1976, vol. ii, p. 144.

12. Michael Holroyd, *Lytton Strachey, The Years of Achievement*, London, 1968, p. 112.

13. *Ibid.*, p. 538.

14. *Journal*, 1954, Preface by Murry, p. x. 'The fragments from 1904 to 1912 . . . appeared to have escaped destruction by pure accident'. They were filled notebooks, not fragments; and they survived because KM retained them.

15. Turnbull MS. accession no. 97306.

16. Account by Mrs G. G. Robieson (Edie Bendall) 1946. Morris MS. (in possession of Mrs Susan Graham, Auckland, New Zealand).

17. Alpers, p. 99.

18. Mantz, p. 309.

19. Tom L. Mills moved from Wellington in 1907 to edit the *Feilding Star*, in which he established a Saturday literary supplement. Mills reviewed *In a German Pension* in his supplement of 6 October 1912, saying of KM 'Katherine Mansfield – who, by the way, wrote some things for the STAR supplement, some five years ago, before leaving for London'. The New Zealand National Library file of the *Star* lacks the relevant volumes; the file of the *Star* in the Feilding Public

Library lacks almost all the supplements, which being half news-sheet size were apparently not bound in. I think these early KM 'things' are gone for ever. I have hunted everywhere.

20. KM to Vera. Turnbull MS.

21. Personal communication from two of KM's contemporaries.

22. KM to Sylvia Payne, March 1908. Turnbull MS.

23. KM to Vera, January 1908. Turnbull MS.

24. KM to Sylvia Payne. Same letter as note 22. Turnbull MS.

25. KM to Harold Beauchamp, July 1922. *Letters*, 1928, vol. ii, p. 232, where Rubi Seddon appears only as 'R'. Her full name is on the typescript copy of the letter deposited by Beauchamp in the Turnbull Library. Harold Beauchamp's grandson, the late Andrew Bell (Canada) received all of KM's letters to her father as a bequest. He informed me that, without his knowledge, they found their way to an American collector. These letters – of critical importance – remain unavailable.

26. Personal communication from Mrs Maude Morris of Auckland (who was one of the women on the committee at the time).

27. KM to Sylvia Payne. Same letter as note 22. Turnbull MS.

28. See 'An Ideal Family' (first collected in *The Garden Party*), where the tennis parties are set in the recognizable 'corner house' in Fitzherbert Terrace (thinly disguised as 'fashionable Harcourt Avenue').

29. KM to Vera, undated, but on internal evidence early 1908. Turnbull MS.

30. Charlotte (Chaddie) Beauchamp to Sylvia Payne, 14 October 1907 (KM's birthday). Text printed in Alpers, p. 89.

31. *Journal*, 1954, pp. 14-15. Murry omitted the words after 'unintellectual head' and gave no indication that he had altered the text of the notebook.

32. *Journal*, 1954, p. 22. The notebook to which this and the previous note refers (Turnbull MS. accession no. 97273) was begun by KM 14 July 1906 in London, carried to New Zealand, completed during 1907, and brought back to London in 1908.

33. KM appears on the Wellington Technical School register as 'Beauchamp, K. Registration number 903'. Her name was entered in May for Commercial Subjects. The names of two future managing directors are on the same page. For an account of my discovery of this enrolment see: Ian A. Gordon, 'Warmth and Hydrangeas; Katherine Mansfield's Wellington Years,' *New Zealand Listener*, 8 May 1976, pp. 22-3.

34. KM to Vera, undated but clearly after KM's enrolment at the Technical school. Vera was in Sydney from late in 1907 till some time into 1908, visiting family friends. KM wrote to her regularly and Vera (the late Mrs Macintosh Bell of Ottawa) retained the letters, which are now in the Turnbull Library.

35. 'I spend a large part of [these days] tapping out my new *long* story or *short* novel on my little Corona' (KM to Harold Beauchamp 28/7/1922). After KM's death, her Corona Portable was used for many years by LM, who then presented it to the Turnbull Library.

36. KM was a fanatical keeper of accounts, even as a schoolgirl. Her 1906 notebook records such items as 'tarts 6d; buns 6d' and the pattern continued throughout her life. Turnbull MS. accession no. 97287 is a complete weekly household account book covering 1914-16 recording such items as 'safety pins for Jack 9d' and sums 'lent to Jack'. Several of her diaries have quite sophisticated balance sheets in the final pages. The basic cost of the Urewera trip was met by Harold Beauchamp, but KM kept meticulous accounts of her own out-of-pocket-expenses – see Appendix.

37. I was told this recently by KM's sister Jeanne (Mrs Renshaw).

38. KM to Vera, undated. Late 1907/early 1908. Turnbull MS. KM thought it an 'excellent scheme'.

39. Harold Beauchamp *Reminiscences and Recollections*, privately printed, New Plymouth, New Zealand, 1937

40. Her allowance was £2 per week in 1908, raised to £3 per week in 1916. In 1919 Beauchamp settled £200 per annum on Vera, Jeanne and Chaddie and £300 a year on KM. KM's allowance was paid monthly through the Bank of New Zealand, London. There are records of cash gifts at Christmas and other payments. Source: KM's accounts, Beauchamp's Instructions to the Bank of New Zealand, London (Turnbull MSS.).

41. A partial text of 'The Scholarship' was printed in the *Scrapbook*, 1939, pp. 93-100. The only full text of this story appears in *Undiscovered Country*, 1974, pp. 253-8.

42. *Journal*, 1954, p. 157.

43. Mantz (and Murry), 1933, p. 333.

44. Cf. *Poems by Katherine Mansfield*, London, 1923, Introductory Note, p. xiii – 'he [the editor of the *New Age*] wanted her to write nothing but satirical prose'.

2 (Text)

1. Walt Whitman: KM was probably reminded of the 'youthful sinewy races' and 'tan-faced children' of the opening verses of *Pioneers! O Pioneers!*

2. toi-toi: The Maori name for the *Cortaderia*, a tall plant with feathery fronds.

3. willow: This willow-fringed site by the Esk River is still used as a camping ground. The party camped here on the return journey 14 December 1907.

4. holes . . . pinholes: *Journal*, 1954, reads 'lilies . . . primroses'.

5. cheque: KM's spelling of 'check'. She was a banker's daughter.

6. great barn of a place: The trains had no dining-cars, and meals were eaten in haste at crowded refreshment stations like Woodville or Kaitoke between Wellington and Hastings.

7. manuka: Flowering bush (*leptospermum scoparium*) common in scrub country. KM wrote a poem on the manuka flower later in the notebook.

8. the organ pipes: KM's description of a stand of what an annotated road-map of the old Napier-Taupo road calls 'huge burnt trees, reminders of earlier eruptions'.

9. the feeling: I.e. of the hot water in the mineral bath. *Journal,* 1954 has the nonsense reading 'felling'.

10. Maori: *Journal, 1954,* reads 'Mary'.

11. camp by the river: This was only a lunch-time stop. The camp for that evening was 'on a peninsula' at Rangitaiki.

12. a *great* pa-man: In Beauchamp family slang a 'pa-man' was a 'real man'. KM's brother Leslie, in a 1915 letter-diary to his parents, called the chief engineer of the ship in which he was travelling 'a true pa-man' (Turnbull MS.).

13. biograph show: The 'biograph' (the earliest name for the cinema) was a new entertainment in the music-halls during KM's London schooldays.

14. a cure (nineteenth-century slang): An eccentric (possibly from 'curious').

15. Miss Wood's eggs: Miss Clara Wood had charge of the Queen's College boarders when KM was at school in London.

16. E ta – Haeremai te kai: Maori for 'Friend, the food is welcome'.

17. ti pore: Maori tree name for *cordyline terminalis*, one of the cabbage-tree group.

18. straight road in a sort of basin of stony mountains: *Journal,* 1954, makes nonsense of the passage by reading 'strange road . . . strong underbrush'. The road to the Troutbeck Station ran alongside a curve of the Whirinaki River, which the early survey maps show at this point was 'reserved for shingle purposes'. KM's 'stony mountains' were great piles of river shingle.

19. *His brother Albert*: Alfred and Albert Warbrick (English father, Maori mother) belonged to a notable family of the Arawa tribe. Both played for the Maori rugby team that toured Britain in 1888. KM, after her return to London, planned in December 1908 to write a novel with a New Zealand heroine, who would be half-English half-Maori. She concluded her note on this plan 'Bring into it Warbrick the guide'. Cf. *Journal*, 1954, p. 38.

20. *Rua tore up the summons*: The Te Whaiti District Constable's *Diary of Duty and Occurrences, 1907*. The *Diary* is now in the National Archives, Wellington, to which it was transferred by the Police Department.

21. huia feathers: The prized tail-feathers of the huia, worn by old-time Maoris as a badge of rank, have become mere dress-ornaments.

22. the built place for koumara and potato: The Maori storehouse ('pataka'), raised above the ground to exclude animals, for the storage of food, including the 'kumara' (sweet potato).

23. kits: Baskets of plaited flax (used by Maoris for food-storage and general carrying purposes).

24. H. G. Wells: The early pages of *The Food of the Gods*, 1904, was illustrated with zig-zag diagrams. KM saw a resemblance to the pattern of the young bracken leaf – which in its early stage does resemble 'a string of beads'.

25. black curls: KM noted several times the long hair worn by Rua's male followers. Mantz, p.295, gives this 'great fellow' the name Feropa, but this is due to a misreading of the text.

26. We play 'Nga maui' with the Maori children: Mantz, p. 293 makes nonsense by reading 'we pick Ngamoni (sweet potatoes)'. The source of the misreading was presumably Murry, since *Journal*, 1954, has the same misreading and the same mistranslation of the Maori. String-games (or cats' cradles) were associated with the Maori ancestral god Maui and were called 'te whai wawewawe o Maui' or (in short) 'nga maui' (i.e. 'the Maui

103

games'). KM was playing string-games with the children – and, with her usual linguistic skill, got the Maori term right. See J. C. Andersen *Maori String Games*, Wellington, 1920, pp. 81, 83.

27. koe-koea (Maori): The feather was from the long-tailed cuckoo, a migrant bird from the Pacific.

28. the Pareheru [hill]: This place-name is not recorded in the list published by the New Zealand Geographical Board and does not appear on the one-inch New Zealand Topographical Map Series, presumably because the road from Waiotapu to Rotorua now by-passes it. But it features in the 1893 Murray's *Handbook for Travellers in New Zealand* as a starred tourist attraction, offering an 'extensive view' of the eruption-shattered mountain Tarawera. It is now the Pareheru Scenic Reserve on the old coach road (now Waimunga Road), Map Reference N85/812070.

29. Whaka: KM, like most New Zealanders, used this shortened form for Whakarewarewa, the main area of thermal and geyser activity at Rotorua.

30. Tom: T. E. Y. Seddon, M.P. was a regular visitor to Rotorua, where he stayed with his Maori friend, Peter Buck. The late Mr Seddon told me how he found 'Kathleen' in tears and took her to lunch.

31. Vera has definitely left: KM's older sister Vera had gone to visit family friends in Sydney, remaining there till after KM left for London. KM's letters to her during this period are now in the Turnbull Library, and have been used in the Introduction.

32. Deepa: Beauchamp family slang, a variation on 'pa-man'. See note 12.

33. Te nakohi: I.e. tena koe ('greeting!'). KM's spelling of Maori is usually accurate. Her spelling suggests she picked this phrase up by ear only.

34. church: KM drew a small cross, which I transcribe as 'church'.

35. Millais' Ophelia: This famous picture, with its rendering of water and flowers, was from 1897-1909 in the Tate Gallery, and KM evidently saw it during her London schooldays.

36. Maeterlinck: The records of the General Assembly Library, Wellington, show that KM borrowed several works by him 1907-8.

37. Wagner: *Journal*, 1954, misses the Rhinemaiden imagery by reading this as 'Wapi', which Murry presumably imagined was some Maori.

38. terza: The young KM often thought in terms of music performance in her writing. The night-scene is a trio (terza). In the following entry, the morning is a 'duet for two oboes'. She had not yet finally decided to abandon her cello for the art of writing.

39. thudding of a paddle wheel . . . dragon's Mouth: The 'Dragon's Mouth' was the name given to one of the Wairakei geysers. Nearby was the 'Donkey Engine', which produced a sound that KM would recognize from hearing paddle steamers on Wellington Harbour.

40. Tannhauser: the green grotto under the Huka Falls reminded KM of a spectacular London production of Wagner's opera.

41. under her: KM's text has these two words transposed.

42. a better shelter: the expedition's baggage-waggon had a large tarpaulin cover to protect the luggage, under which KM sheltered.

43. 1946 account by Mrs G. G. Robieson. Morris MS., Auckland.

Sources & Acknowledgements

All citation and references in my Introduction are documented in detail in the Notes. The running narrative in my headnotes to KM's text is based on a variety of sources, written and oral. The late Mr G. N. Morris, of Auckland, collected much information from KM's contemporaries, and I am indebted to Mrs Morris and her daughter Mrs Susan Graham for access to this material: notably a timetable and itinerary for the trip made about 1939 by Mr and Mrs Webber; letters from Mrs Webber of later dates; a 1942 account of KM supplied by Miss Margaret Amelia Parker (Millie of the notebook); a 1946 account of KM on her return from the trip provided by Mrs G. G. Robieson (EKB); The Webbers and Miss Parker are the ultimate sources for the photographs, prints of which were made available by the Turnbull Library. The Library also holds a later (1956) account of the trip by Mrs Webber. The various accounts, written many years after the event, have some inaccuracies and discrepancies due to faulty memory.

Further information has been derived from the *Hawkes Bay Almanacs* of the period; the contemporary issues of the *New Zealand Post Office Directories*; the *Cyclopedia of New Zealand*, especially vols ii and iv, 1897-1908; the New Zealand Railways Department; the New Zealand Police Department; the National Archives, Wellington, the Land and Survey Department, Hamilton, which provided me with copies of early survey maps. I am grateful to Mrs

Elaine Price of Rotorua, who sought out for me information on the Troutbeck Station, Galatea, and on the Warbrick family; to Mr B. Kernott who helped me with the Maori; to Dr Alan North, who was in practice for many years at Te Whaiti; and to Mrs Margaret Scott for consultations on KM's sometimes very difficult script.

The following books were of particular use: Elsdon Best *Tuhoe*, 1925; A. Warbrick *Adventures in Geyserland*, 1934; *Handbook of the Urewera National Park*, 1975. A near-contemporary guide-book *Murray's Handbook for Travellers in New Zealand*, 1893, with its detailed maps and 'tourist information' still valid in 1907 – but otherwise quite irrecoverable today – was of particular value. I am especially grateful for my own (quite unwitting) foresight in having camped along the greater part of KM's route before highway improvement made that impossible.

Finally, a unique series of debts: to those of KM's contemporaries with whom I have had many conversations – her sister Mrs Jeanne Renshaw; Mrs G. G. Robieson (EKB); Mrs G. N. Morris; and the following now deceased: Mrs Edith Miller; Mr Siegfried Eichelbaum; Mr T. E. Y. Seddon.